WHAT DID I DO TOMORROW?

L. P. DAVIES

What Did I Do Tomorrow?

DOUBLEDAY & COMPANY, INC., GARDEN CITY, NEW YORK, 1973

All of the characters in this book are fictitious, and any resemblance
to actual persons, living or dead, is purely coincidental.

ISBN: 0-385-07807-2
Library of Congress Catalog Card Number 72–89300
Copyright © 1972 by L. P. Davies
All Rights Reserved
Printed in the United States of America
First Edition in the United States of America

1

HE HAD BEEN ASLEEP and was not yet wholly awake. The afternoon sun on his face, the warm June breeze stirring his yellow-brown hair, Howell Trowman strolled along the balustrade-edged terrace that overlooked the sunken tennis courts alongside the main school building, reliving the scene of a dream, of a series of vivid dreams, rather, strung together like pearls on a thread. Dreams that had been alive with colours, sounds, sensations.

A circle of tiny people on tiny chairs, and he one of them. Singing together in tiny cracked voices under the paper garlands and tinsel of the first Christmas he could remember, as far back as memory would take him. Nothing before that, no gurgling-in-pram memories. How old? Kindergarten. Say four, then.

And then the soft stickiness of modelling clay, and its faint clove smell. A zoo . . . No, a circus. An elephant with huge ears and a marvellous curled trunk; a snake—that had been easy to make; a man with a whip that wouldn't stay put, but kept drooping. All set out on a small square of wood. He could still smell the lavender of the teacher as she had leaned over him, feel the cushiony softness of her breast. Six, he must have been then.

And then the time—seven now—when he had fallen off the

farm gate. Memorable, not for the great height of the fall, but because of the long splinter that had embedded its two inches or more of blackness in the firm flesh of his calf, and the satisfying way in which he had been able to draw it out, painlessly, with only one globule of blood, like pulling a sword from a sheath.

And then his first day at Budders—otherwise Buddleigh Hall School for the sons of Gentlemen—a week after his twelfth birthday, over five years ago now. A fearful place of strange faces, strange smells, even stranger customs. A first night indoctrination had been a ceremony involving soot, ashes and castor oil.

Still with his dreams, Howell turned the corner of the building and dropped down the three stone steps to the lower and wider terrace that fronted the school. And there the unusual sight of cars, perhaps a score of them, drawn up in a rough line on the large expanse of forecourt, changed the substance of his thoughts and finally drove the dream pictures away. The cars belonged to those parents who had been able to accept, or had felt in the mood for accepting, the Head's usual invitation to Founder's Day lunch. Hands in the pockets of his dark blue blazer, Howell paused to watch a small party of those parents being led through the rose garden by one of the junior masters, probably on their way to inspect the new addition to the East Wing. A tall dark-haired youth with an almost Italianate complexion came through the clipped yellow privet bushes of the so-called Formal garden to mount the steps up to the terrace. Martin Debroy was about the same age as Howell, in the same top senior form, and occupied one of the small private rooms set aside for senior prefects, that next door to Howell's.

"What-ho, Howie, old son." His teeth, when he smiled, were of a remarkable whiteness against the dark olive of his narrow, high-boned face. "And a happy Founder's Day, nineteen sixty-nine, to you. How come you're frittering the golden hours away up here instead of being out at the nets getting in trim for this evening?"

"I've dropped out of the side to give Bennett a place."

Taking his hands from his pockets, Howell rested his elbows on the balustrade. "Let him get the feel of things before the Old Boys' match."

"And very noble of you. But then they do say there's nothing like cricket for bringing out the best in a chap." Debroy joined Howell in leaning on the weathered grey stone. "So you are leaving at the end of term?"

His gaze remote, Howell nodded briefly. "Nothing to be gained by hanging on till Christmas."

"I'm with you there. Decided yet what you're going to do, Howie?"

Howell rested his chin on his clasped hands. "Not yet."

"A bit tricky," the other said sympathetically. "If you go off to snob it at Oxford, like your old man wants, you upset the old lady. And if you do as she wants, and go into the family business, then you'll come up against the old man. Either way you're in dead stook. It's a pity the three of you can't put your heads together and come up with something to satisfy everyone. But you not supposed to be knowing about your old man's state of health rather puts the kibosh on it. How do you feel about it yourself, Howie? If it was left to you, which would you rather do?"

Howell didn't want to talk about it, not even to Debroy. He had come out here to be alone, to try to think, to try to work something out before his parents arrived. He had the sudden feeling that his surge of resentment at Debroy's intrusion wasn't new, that this same conversation had taken place, word for word, once before.

"What I feel doesn't matter," he replied, and was conscious of sounding smugly self-sacrificing. He added quickly, awkwardly: "You know what I mean, Mick."

"Yeah. How is the old man? Dicky heart, didn't you say?"

Howell nodded. "I only know what Mother told me when she came at half term. She doesn't mention it in her letters because he usually adds a bit to them and he might read what she'd written."

"Must be a bit tricky for you when you're with him, having to pretend you don't know anything," Debroy said sympa-

7

thetically, and nodded his sleek dark head in the direction of the concourse of cars. "I take it they haven't rolled up yet?"

Howell twisted his wrist to bring his watch into view. "Should get here about three. They were stopping at Cambridge for an early lunch."

"Far to come? I always forget where your family estates are."

"Gretton. Not far from Epsom."

"Where the salts come from. I remember you saying, now. Right up your old man's street, as it were." Debroy grinned. "Which reminds me, you won't be the only one handing in his cards at term-end. Yours truly put himself on the transfer list this morning."

"You did?" Howell glanced sideways at his companion. "University?"

"In a way. Part-timing. My folks had to scrape the barrel to send me here. Even if I got a grant they wouldn't be able to back me through university full time. No, I've managed to fix myself up with a firm of manufacturing chemists." Debroy looked down at his folded arms. "Solmex. They'll subsidise me through university—red-brick—Manchester, probably, God help me. And I sign an agreement to work at least three years for them when I get my degree."

Straightening, Howell smiled. "So you're going to work for the enemy."

"I was waiting for that." Debroy became intensely dramatic. "Will this mean the end of our great friendship?" And then was serious. "Are Solmex and your old man's firm that much against each other, Howie?"

"I wouldn't know." Howell shrugged. "I suppose, for all Dad says, they're really no more against each other than any other two firms that sell the same sort of things. I've heard Dad say many times that whenever he brings out a new line, Solmex are bound to copy it and bring out their own. If I know anything, it works the other way round as well."

"I can see it all," Debroy mused. "One day, there I'll be, supervising a machine turning out laxative pills, while you'll be sitting in the gaffer's office, making your millions faster than I'm making my pills. You a millionaire, me a humble pill-maker. Will you take over from your old man when the day comes, or is there anyone else in front of you? Didn't you once say something about an uncle somewhere?"

"Uncle Wilf." Howell nodded. "Only he's not really my uncle, just an old friend of the family. He and Aunt Meg have always been around. They don't have any kids of their own. You know how it is. He and Dad actually started the firm, way back in the year dot. Only it was so shaky in those days Uncle Wilf packed it in, and then came back when things picked up. He's Dad's general manager now."

Debroy nodded his understanding. "He could take over if anything were to happen to your old man before you're old enough to become the gaffer."

"I don't think—" Howell started unthinkingly, and then broke off rather abruptly. What Mother had told him about the way Dad's mind worked had been just between the two of them.

Debroy slanted a sardonic eyebrow. "Because I'm now one of the enemy?"

"For Pete's sake," Howell said, embarrassed, and looked at his watch again. "Nearly half two. Just about time for a shower before they get here."

They walked back along the sun-warm terrace. The tennis courts were all occupied now. White shirts, the sweet smell of freshly cut grass, sticky over-sweet lemonade, Alma Mater. Howell looked up at the ivy-covered school wall. All corny things; things to laugh at, to sneer at. Things he was going to miss like the devil no matter which way he chose.

"My people aren't coming this time," Debroy offered to break the silence. "He can't get away from business, she's on the sick list. I don't know about Eileen . . . You've never met my sister, have you, Howie? Dark like me, only prettier. So they say. I wouldn't mind having a millionaire for a brother-in-law. How about it?"

And once again Howell had the same strange feeling that all this, right down to the very last detail, had happened before. They had a name for it . . . Déjà vu. That I-have-been-here-before feeling. Memories of past incarnations, said those who went in for that sort of thing. A phenomenon caused by one

9

part of the brain working a fraction slower than the rest, suggested those scientifically inclined. Because, explained the more down-to-earth types, the present sequence of events is in fact very similar to some sequence out of the past. And that had to be the explanation now.

Take one Founder's Day, and you had them all. Always sunshine—Howell couldn't recall one when it had rained or even been overcast. Always the same feel to the day, right from the moment of waking; always the same cars down there on the forecourt, the same collection of dutiful parents and Old Boys, the same faces year after year, never seeming to get older.

And that sameness—that feeling of sameness, rather—was bound to be more pronounced than ever this year because for a long time now, ever since Mother had visited him at half term to tell him about Dad's illness, he had been thinking about the coming Founder's Day, knowing that it—today, now—would be his last one, that he would be leaving at the end of term, in only three weeks' time; that he would have to have his decision ready—whether to go to Oxford to take his degree, as Dad wanted, or do as Mother wanted and go straight into the firm. For Dad's sake . . .

"—Last year, Howell, when he was ill and I wrote telling you he had been overworking, that was his first attack—his heart . . .

"He doesn't know how serious his condition is. The doctors say it wouldn't help him to know. He must be persuaded to give up work in a year at the outside. Then he'll stand a chance of living another ten years, perhaps longer. But if he carries on working, driving himself—

"Uncle Wilf? No, darling, your father would never consider handing over to him. It would be different if Wilfred really were your uncle, but he isn't, only a very close friend, and for your father, that isn't enough. It has to be his own flesh and blood. You know that. Young as you are, darling, he would trust you. Because you are his son. Twelve months, if you work very hard. That should be long enough, must be long enough for you to learn to take his place. It's up to you, darling. Show him you can do it. Then, with the doctors' help, we can persuade him to retire."

Just like that. Howell stared grimly in front. It wasn't right that he should be the one to have to make the decision. It wasn't fair of Mother to have dumped it in his lap like that. Maybe she had thought she knew what she was doing. First lesson in becoming a man . . .

Debroy's voice brought him back to the present. They were crossing the polished expanse of the big hall, passing the stage, the stacks of folded chairs and the gilt-on-walnut memorial list of Old Boys who had died in two world wars.

"The way I see it," Debroy observed, "you're getting yourself all worked up over nothing. Look, if your old man's as bad as they say he is, and he's got to pack it in, and he won't hand over to anyone but you, then surely there's only the one thing you can do, go straight into the firm like your old lady wants. Though for the life of me I can't see him handing over the reins of a whacking great concern like Trowman Chemicals to you after only a year. Strewth, you'd still be only eighteen."

They started to climb the staircase that curved up from one corner of the hall. Sunlight from high windows laid patterns of gold over the mottled grey marble.

"Nineteen," Howell corrected. "I'll be eighteen next month. Mother's idea is that I work like the clappers for a year, to show Dad what I can do, and then we sort of get together with the doctors and talk him into retiring."

They had reached the row of doors that led to the six tiny rooms reserved for head prefects.

"Well then," Debroy said. "Where's the problem?"

Howell leaned against the closed door of his room. "You've met my father, but you don't know him, Mick. A one-track mind. What he sets out to do he finishes. Which is how he got where he is today. For as long as I can remember he's had his heart set on me going to Oxford. Probably because he never had anything like that himself. He left school to start work when he wasn't quite thirteen."

"And that makes him so different?" The other was scathing. "Hell, if we're to believe all we see on the telly, everyone who is someone started off life either flogging newspapers in the gutter, blacking boots or bouncing their bones against overhead coal seams."

"You wouldn't understand. Other people get notions. Dad gets obsessions. The day I was born he put my name down for prep school. Then this—" Howell's gesture took in the panelled walls of the corridor and the line of framed photographs of ancient cricket elevens and rowing eights. "All part of the same thing. And whatever Dad starts, he finishes. Or else—" He shrugged.

Debroy finished the sentence for him. "Or else cuts up rough, blows his top and anything else you can think of. I'm beginning to see daylight. You think that going against his wishes would really start things humming, and that, in his state of health, wouldn't be very clever. Is that what's in your mind, Howie?"

Mother had been very cool and calm about that possibility. *A chance we'll just have to take, darling. We'll just have to, don't you see? The lesser of two evils. He only may have another attack if you go against his wishes and make him angry. But if you go to university instead of joining the firm, and he keeps on working at his present pace—* No need for her to finish the sentence.

"*But the doctors can't be sure,*" he had protested half-heartedly.

"*They're as sure as the finest specialists in the country can be, darling.*" Harley Street, of course.

"*He could turn awkward and refuse to let me join the firm until I'm older, until I've got my degree,*" he had offered with even less conviction.

"*He could—*" Mother had thought of everything. *But I don't for one minute think he would. Your father's not made that way, Howell. He's not vindictive. And we both know how he has his heart set on you taking over from him one day. He wouldn't do anything to risk that not happening.*"

"Knowing Dad, he'll blow his top right enough," Howell said. "Yes, that's what's in my mind, Mick."

The other folded his arms and leaned one shoulder against the wall.

"Tricky," he said sympathetically. "Either way, things could turn sour. And if anything did happen—you know—you'd blame yourself and you'd have to live with it, and that wouldn't be much fun. And everyone else would blame you too. A pity we can't see into the future."

And again, for the third time now, Howell had the same eerie feeling that all this had happened before, so that he knew what was to come next, that at any moment Andy would come along the corridor with his peculiar, clumsy long-legged lope, swinging a towel, his hair wet from the showers. He would stop and—

Swinging a towel in time to his stride, his wild fair hair for once under control, plastered darkly down with water, Andrew Brett came along the corridor. An ugly face his, until he smiled, and then satanic-slanted brows, witch-pointed chin, flattened nose and too-large mouth took on a kind of impish, little-boy appeal.

Flicking his towel in greeting, then draping it scarf-fashion round his neck, he treated them to that transforming smile, asking generally: "Why so serious? Some kind of conference in progress?"

"Not that you'd notice," Debroy retorted with no great warmth. He and Brett never had got on all that well together. He nodded at Howell. "Be seeing you." And went into his room.

Brett pulled a face. "Did I butt into something?"

"Nothing special." Howell glanced at his watch. Talking, the time had passed more quickly than he had imagined. He would have to do without a shower.

Brett, grave now, wiped the front of his hair with one end of his scarf-towel, asking: "Made your mind up yet what you're going to do, Howie?"

Howell shook his head. "I've thought that much I'm going round in circles."

Brett tried to be helpful. "I was thinking, coming along now. Your father's a sensible type—he must be, to have got where he is." He sounded to be very much in earnest, as if he had indeed been giving the matter a great deal of thought.

"Why shouldn't he be told outright just how sick he really is, and then left to work out for himself what's best to be done?"

The short time left before his parents were due to arrive, Howell wanted to spend alone with his problem. He didn't want to talk about it any more. All the same, he felt grateful to Brett for trying to be helpful.

"It's not as easy as all that, Andy. The doctors say that he just hasn't got the temperament for that sort of thing. Knowing how bad he is would only make matters worse. He'd get as angry with himself for getting in his own way as he.would with anyone else. He'd thwart himself into another attack; that's what one specialist told Mother. Thanks all the same." He opened the door of his room. "I'd best get tidied up before they arrive."

But Brett still had something to say. "You won't forget, Howie?"

With his own problem occupying all of his thoughts, Howell had forgotten. He remembered now that Brett had asked him if he would speak to Dad about finding a place for him in the firm.

So: "I won't forget, Andy. Let's see—you won't be leaving till summer next year."

Brett nodded eagerly. "Not lab work or anything like that. Stinks never was my subject. Advertising or admin. Even travelling. You know."

"I'll sound him out." Howell closed the door. It would be the first time, anyway, he had asked Dad a favour of that kind. He didn't think the old man would cut up rough, even though he always had been dead against the idea of jobs for the boys. Like he had promised Andy, he could but try.

He went to stand by the narrow uncurtained window that overlooked the front of the school. More cars had come to join those down there on the forecourt, one a snazzy white sports job. He wondered whose parents that belonged to. Very soon now and Dad's ageless black Austin Princess would come nosing its way through the gates.

Howell turned his back on the window to face the room. A tiny, carpetless cell of a place, walls a workhouse green. Box-like wardrobe; hospital bed; apology for a dressing-table; a couple of book-shelves; uncomfortable straight-backed chair. Always smelling of floor wax and the antiseptic they used in the locker room—a smell that managed to find its way all over the school.

Turning the chair to face the window he sat down. By raising himself a fraction he could bring the gates into view. Through them, very soon now . . . He would go down to meet them, Mother in blue—always blue—Dad in his idea of country wear: tweed suit and hand-knitted tie. At the first opportunity—and if there wasn't one, she'd make it—Mother would take him on one side to ask if he was ready to go straight into the firm; she would be so sure that that was what he would have decided to do. And Dad . . . If he knew anything about the old man he would have Oxford all laid on, and would have wallowed happily in every moment of that laying-on. Digs arranged; an allowanced fixed; maybe even train times all worked out. And his colleagues and cronies sick to death of listening to him going on about his son who was going up to Oxford.

Howell stared moodily down at his feet. A pity we can't take a look into the future, Mick had said. Or something like that. It was a pity all right. If only it were possible. To find out what the outcome had been of whatever decision he would have to reach within the next few minutes. A spot of time travelling. Or just crystal gazing. *I see a tall dark stranger* . . . He pulled himself up. Instead of letting his mind wander he should be concentrating on what he was going to tell Mother and Dad when they showed up. And what the hell was he going to tell them? Which was it to be—

And then it happened.

Afterwards, looking back, he was to be absolutely sure in his own mind that there had been no time, not even the smallest fraction of a second, when he had not been fully aware of himself and his surroundings; that he had not even closed his eyes so much as to blink; that there had been no gap, no hiatus of any kind between his being in one place and then in another. No blackout, no memory lapse, not even a momentary break in awareness.

He didn't feel the texture of the chair change beneath him,

but was aware that it had done so, hard wood changing to smooth cool leather. He saw the shape of the window waver and melt and become rows of books in a bookcase. He watched the quality of the light change, from the clear golden of sunlight to the artificial light of a desk lamp. No windows to this new room in which he found himself, or if there were, then they were behind the wine-red drapes to the right of the bookcase.

His feet sank into the rich pile of a russet-red carpet. In front of him was a desk, a splendid, massive affair of gleaming dark-red wood, the lamp at one end, a scattering of papers— perhaps an open file—in the middle, a small wooden filing box at the other end. Pictures on the walls: heavy-framed portraits and seascapes. In one corner, mounted on a pedestal, a bronze statue of some kind of nymph or dryad.

There was no sense of fear.

He was in another place and, because he felt himself to be different, altered, he knew himself to be in a different time.

2

THERE WAS NO FEELING OF FEAR, no apprehension of any kind, only a calm acceptance of the fact that something had happened, and a sense of wonderment at the seeming strangeness of that happening. By some means or other—impossible though the thing was—he had been transported bodily and instantaneously from one place and time and set down in another place at another time. That much Howell felt certain of. Even in the first few minutes he felt he knew what had happened, why it had happened, but not how. A time for thinking, for figuring it all out, would come later. Now he had to come to terms with the new present.

He was sitting—no, lounging—in the depths of a large leather-covered armchair on what was obviously the visitors' side of the huge desk. The chair on the other side was empty, swivelled sideways, giving—for some reason he couldn't be sure of—the impression that whoever had sat there had risen only moments ago, had left the room for some reason or other, leaving by the door over on the right—it stood ajar—and would be returning at any moment. To take up a conversation where it had been left off. A conversation that Howell would be unable to cope with. Which certainly meant that within minutes of the someone who had occupied that chair returning to occupy it, that someone, whoever he or she was, would discover that something had come over the person with whom he or she had been talking.

And that, Howell reasoned, still calmly enough for all his sense of urgency, would create a very dicey situation to say the least. One that he could only attempt to cover by offering the explanation that he had suffered a sudden and unaccountable loss of memory. And who in their right mind would buy a story like that? There was only one thing for him to do, and that was get the hell out of it. All right, so the absent someone returning to find his visitor flown would think it queer. But that would be nothing to what he or she would think it that visitor had stayed.

Howell had to struggle to push himself up out of the cloying depths of the chair. Behind him was another door, this one closed. He went quickly across to it, not wasting any time on the rest of the contents of the quite large room, receiving the vague impression of a set of cupboards against one wall—perhaps filing cabinets—and another bookcase, this seeming to be filled with books of reference—too large anyway for ordinary fiction. Opening the door he peered out. Sunlight filled a large hall, golden-bright after the paler artificial light of the desk lamp, flooding in through the glass panels and transom of the door at the far end. A door that obviously led to the outside.

He made towards it, his feet sinking into the pile of a carpet so deep that it almost possessed the nightmare quality of slowing his pace, holding him back. But this was no dream. He hadn't fallen asleep in his room back at school and was dreaming all this. It was too real. And to confirm that reality he lurched, quite unintentionally, against the side of a monstrous ornate hallstand. There was nothing dreamlike about the stab of pain where a carved knob jabbed against his hip.

The door opened easily at the turn of a large white china knob, closed silently behind him as he stepped outside. Six cream stone steps, stone rails on each side, led down to the pavement. A quiet, sunlit road; no passing traffic, only one or two people walking, but wide enough to have cars parked bumper to bumper on either side. Large, sleek, opulent cars, all of them. Cars to match their surroundings of tall, solidly

18

elegant, utterly respectable Victorian houses, colour-washed white, cream, beige; bow-windowed up to the attics; railings linking four-square gateposts; more steps leading down to discreet basement entrances. Like the seaside boarding houses of Howell's holiday youth, but grander, more dignified, and all—so far as he could see as he walked towards the end of the street where traffic flowed by along a main road—with brass plates mounted on the stone pillars of the doorways; several to each house, polished and gleaming, some so worn their wording was barely discernible—a typing agency, Howell noticed; a Commissioner for Oaths, a Notary Public, another agency of some kind, but mostly solicitors so far as he could tell, firms of lawyers with combinations of anything up to eight names. Long-established, then, to fit in with their surroundings. And at the end of the street, attached breast-high to the railings where they curved to join the main road, was a plate of a different kind, this bearing the name of the street: Gladwyn Place S.W.19.

It came as no great surprise to find he was somewhere in the south-west district of London. The street of one-time select residences, converted now to business and professional use, had suggested a large city. And there had been something about the atmosphere, the general air of the place, that reminded him of past visits to London. So that was it then—London, and in the not too distant future. For, standing on the corner, watching the busy main-road flow of traffic, he was able to recognise and put names to most of the cars that swept by. Only here and there were types that were obviously unfamiliar. If he had to make a guess, he would say he was not more than ten years in the future.

And the time of year. No doubt about that. Warm sunshine and clear blue sky. Summer. About the same time of year as the June he had just left back in 1969. Not that it mattered all that much. Although on second thought it might be just as well if he were to learn as much about his new surroundings as he could before trying to fit into them. That's if he wanted to fit unobtrusively and not start folk off thinking he wasn't quite right in the head. The first thing to do was find a quiet place where he could sit down and think and get himself generally organised before venturing farther afield. Moving to the edge of the pavement he looked along the main road in both directions.

Some distance away on the right the bright green of trees, sandwiched between buildings, suggested the entrance to either a park or public gardens. He started off in that direction, walking along the quite busy pavement past a row of shops. Automatically he noted the time—twenty past eleven—on the ornately gilded clock hanging outside a jeweller's. Equally automatically he lifted his wrist to check with his own watch. Twenty past eleven it is, it agreed. Fair enough, so it was mid-morning here of whatever day it was, in whatever month of whatever year he had landed in.

And then something didn't make sense. His pace slowed. Morning here. Right. But where he had come from it had been something to three in the afternoon. That was the time his watch had been showing before he had been moved bodily here. So how come the time on his watch had changed to match the time here?

He came to a halt in front of a window filled with men's clothing, frowning, trying to figure it out. A stranger in a blue suit frowned back at him from between pyramids of boxed shirts. Howell moved on. And then came to another halt, this one abrupt, as the significance of what he had just seen dawned blindingly on him. Hurriedly he retraced the few steps to the window of gaudy shirt-pyramids to stare with a mixture of fascination and disbelief at the stranger in the blue suit that was his own reflection in the background mirror.

Certainly older—teenage gawkiness replaced by a kind of maturity—no doubt now about this being the future—no taller, but broader, with features that if taken singly were pretty much as they had always been, but if taken collectively, produced a face that was markedly different from the one that had looked back at him from the locker-room mirror only a couple of hours ago.

The hair was still the same faded light brown, but longer than he had been allowed to wear it at school, much longer

20

and thicker, growing low at the back of his neck and brushed straight across from left to right without the familiar parting. His eyes—he leaned forward, seeing they were changed but finding it hard to put his finger on the subtle difference. Just—older. And the same with a nose, his father's nose, that had always been too broad for a narrow face, a mouth that had always been a little too large and set too low above a chin, his mother's soft chin, that would have benefitted by being more pronounced. A very ordinary face—of what?—anything from twenty to thirty years. An indoor face rather than an outdoor one, with an office desk pallor.

And his clothes . . . According to Mother, blue never had been his colour, and so he had never worn it. Greys, always shades of grey. Good cloth, of course, and always made to measure. And now this. Not that he was any judge of clothes, but if he had to make a guess he would say that this suit now had been bought off the peg. A cheap-looking blue suit, loose at the neck, baggy under the armpits. And with it a plain white linen shirt and a dowdy-looking grey tie.

And that was it. The Howell Trowman of an as yet unknown year in the future. It had been a shock to look in the mirror and find his appearance changed, but already he was getting used to the idea, able to make sense of it, able now to find a satisfactory answer to the small puzzle of why the time as shown by his watch should match the time here. Because there were two different watches—no, that wasn't quite right—it was the same watch, but at two different periods in its existence, each telling the time that fitted each existence. The watch he was wearing now was the same one he'd been wearing back at school, only much older. Just like the person wearing it. It was obvious now what had happened. The Howell of "now" had stepped aside to make way for the Howell of 1969, here on a visit to find out what the future held. Science fiction stuff—Howell smiled at that—but there was just no other explanation that fitted the facts. And if he were to tell anyone, they would say he was off his rocker—stark, raving bonkers. Just as well he hadn't hung on in that office place back there to meet the someone the Howell of "now" had been talking to.

But if he wanted to find out what had happened to him in this future—and that had to be why he had been brought here—then he would have to meet and mingle with and talk to people who knew the Howell of "now." And some of those, probably most of them, would be complete strangers to the Howell of 1969.

He'd have to think of some way of handling things. Could he get away with that idea of saying he had lost his memory? Not all of it, just part. "The first thing I knew, there I was, sitting in this posh-looking office. And the last thing I could remember before that was being back in my old room at school." Which didn't sound very convincing. Was it possible for someone to lose a whole slab of memory like that? He didn't know. But whether or not that sort of thing did happen, one thing was for sure—he'd find himself whipped away to a doctor before you could say knife, maybe even dumped in some kind of hospital or institution. What sort of treatment, for Pete's sake, did they dish out to amnesia patients?

He shuddered a little at the word "patients." And it reminded him of something the strangeness of events had driven clean out of mind: what was certainly the chief reason for his having been brought here for a glimpse of the future. A glimpse . . . He wondered how long he would be allowed to stay before being whisked back to his room at school. Perhaps only for a very short time. If he wanted to make sure of finding out what decision he had come to way back in 1969, what the outcome had been, if Father was still alive, then he couldn't afford to waste time, he must get cracking as soon as possible.

Howell turned away from the window and the stranger in the blue suit. Even now, looking down at himself as he walked, lifting his arm, this time to look at his sleeve, seeing the apparent cheapness of the blue cloth, he still found himself thinking of his reflection as someone he didn't know, had only just met for the first time. The body he inhabited might be that of a man getting on for thirty, but what was inside was still himself, unchanged, still a schoolboy of not quite eighteen.

He reached the trees. Not a park, not even a public garden, little more than a short tree-lined walk that linked one street to another. But at the centre of that link the path widened to form a circle; and there were slatted seats there, six of them, three on either side. Two on the left were occupied—an elderly woman on one, by the two bulging shapeless bags at her feet, resting after shopping before starting for home. And on the other an old man in a greasy brown cap who dozed, sitting bolt upright, his chin sinking ever lower over the knuckles of hands clasped about the curved top of his walking stick.

Howell lowered himself to the green slats of the centre one of the facing seats. The woman treated him to a disinterested glance and then resumed her study of that part of the far road that was visible. Perhaps she was waiting for someone. The sound of the traffic had been reduced to little more than a murmur. In the branches above Howell's head an invisible bird whistled the same three notes over and over again. He relaxed, stretching his legs out in front. No, not his legs, those of the Howell of "now." Encased in shiny blue serge and finished off with dusty shoes that a clean would have improved. Nothing like the hand-made shoes he had been wearing back at school.

An alarming notion occurred to him. All the indications so far were that he had come down in the world. And that might mean that as a result of the decision he had had to make way back in 1969, Father had died and the business gone bust. Howell blew silent dismay through pursed lips. But that was jumping to conclusions. The reason he was here was to find out the facts. And the first thing to do was to find out for himself as much about this new Howell as possible. The contents of his pockets would be a good starter.

In one trouser pocket a not over-clean handkerchief and some loose change. The silver was familiar enough, but the bronze seemed to be foreign. Howell frowned in some perplexity at coins he first took to be French centimes, but then, after studying them more closely, saw they were English after all. And then suddenly knew what they were, why they were strange to him, remembering that back in 1969 the public were being slowly prepared for the change over to a decimal currency, that some of the silver coins were already in circulation. And so these were what the new pennies looked like, a hundred of them to a pound. And that meant that this—he had to think—must be at least 1971, for that was to have been the year of conversion. He went through the coins again, this time looking at the dates. A two-penny piece had been minted in 1972. Any advance on '72? No. Right. So now he could say with every degree of certainty that he had moved at least three years into the future. But the body he wore looked to him to be older than twenty-one.

Returning the coins to his pocket he tried that on the other side, this time finding a bunch of keys, three of them, all yale-type, two of the usual size, one smaller; and with them a silver—or what looked to be silver—miniature replica of a car number plate. TYD 463E. Which led him to suppose that the smaller member of the trio was a car ignition key. And the other two? Home, he guessed, and office, and not in any way helpful in the way of establishing a background for himself.

The two outside jacket pockets were empty, but the inside had a wallet to offer: the leather wallet Mother had given him on his seventeenth birthday and was now at least three years older than the last time he had seen it, which had been earlier that same day. Then, so far as he could remember, it had contained amongst other things his driving licence—his first one, taken out the year before—a few postage stamps, a plastic calendar and some money in notes, he wasn't sure how much. He checked the contents now. Six pound notes; unlike the coins, their design had remained the same. A dog-eared snapshot, a photograph of Mother and Dad he hadn't seen before, taken in the garden at home at Ferncroft. The old man didn't look all that well—older, worried. A piece of paper, a leaf from a small memo pad, it looked like, with a name and address on it in a clear, round childish hand: Christine Martin, 19a Bessemer Terrace S.11. And apart from a strip of stamp edging, that was all the wallet held. Little enough to be of any help.

The paper bearing the name and address looked to be very recent. At least it was still clean and white, not tinged with brown as paper kept in a leather wallet is likely to become

24

after a time. And who the deuce was Christine Martin, and why had she, or someone else, written out her address for him?

Replacing the few things in the wallet, Howell slipped it back into his pocket, having added nothing at all to his small store of background knowledge. Leaning back, he glanced across at his companions. The old man still dozed over his stick, the woman still gazed expectantly in the direction of the road. And looking in that direction himself, Howell saw the wire-basket litter container, attached to the trunk of a tree. And among the usual debris of toffee bags, cigarette cartons and ice cream tubs was a roughly folded newspaper. To reach it he would have to get to his feet, walk a few paces and then maybe have to ferret about in the rubbish. And if anyone saw him—and likely the woman would—they'd think he was that poor he couldn't even afford to buy a morning paper. Well, they could think what they damn' well liked.

He carried his trophy back to the bench and opened it out. A small paper—what was the word?—tabloid; easy to handle, to turn the pages even with unsteady fingers. And his were unsteady, but only with eagerness to reach the front page. And reaching it, the headlines took his eye first, even though it was the date and year he was after. Disappointing by their very mediocrity; nothing startling: Injured climber rescued by helicopter from mountain in Lake District; warehouse men threaten to withdraw their labour if wage demands not met; pile-up of vehicles in early morning mist on M1. The sort of stuff he might have read in any newspaper back in 1969. And now . . . He looked at the top of the page. Saturday, July 6, 1974.

So that was it. It might not be today's paper, but it was certainly this year's. 1974. He had expected it to be more than that—somewhere getting on for the eighties. He lifted his gaze to the opposite trees while he did his small mental calculation. Five years into the future; five years older. Twenty-three. That was how old he was now. At least, he corrected himself, that was the age of the body he was now using. Twenty-three. Seeing it in the mirror he had expected it to be more than that. It had looked older. "It" . . . He grimaced at the way he had taken to thinking of himself in five years' time as "it" instead of "he." "He," then. He had given the impression of looking older than twenty-three. He wasn't sure why. Something about the eyes, he fancied, touching their corners now. Harder, lined. Worry lines perhaps, rather than age. And what sort of worries might this new "he" have? The one he had already thought of: the old man dead and the firm gone bust. Unlikely—at least the going bust part—but always possible. And the old man dead. That was very much on the cards, the way things had been back in '69. Family worries rather than business. Family . . . And another thought occurred to him, one that caused him to lower the newspaper and stare ahead in consternation. For all he knew he might be married. *Married.* Oh, Lord . . .

He didn't realise he had exclaimed aloud, but he must have done, for the woman had turned her head to stare at him and the old man had opened his eyes. Howell lifted his newspaper to hide himself away from their combined startled gazes. Embarrassed, he turned the pages. And there was an advertisement, a half-page spread that must have cost the earth, for Lady Jane Silver Cosmetics. And to reassure him that it still belonged to the old firm, and the old firm still had its headquarters in the same old place, there it was along the bottom: A product of Trowman Chemicals Ltd. of Gretton. He blew a small silent sigh of relief. At least that part was all right.

He closed the paper. The sporting news was on the back page, on the back few pages. Including racing results. Three pages of race meetings and all the winners. Dozens of them. The only time he backed horses was for the Derby or the National. He had never won a sausage in his life. And now, here—here they all were. Tomorrow's winners. Well, some distant tomorrow. Armed with this knowledge, starting with no more than say a fiver, it would be possible to win a small fortune. All he had to do was keep the paper in a safe place until five years had rolled by—

But that wouldn't work. He wouldn't be able to take the paper back with him. It would be left behind along with everything else belonging to the borrowed body he was using. Damn . . . Well, at least he could memorise as many of the winners as possible and then write them down as soon as he was returned to his own time. And the stock market, the price of shares . . . But all that would have to come later. If only he knew how long it would be before he was whipped back to his own time. Could be he was only to be allowed a few hours to find out what had happened as a result of the decision he had had to make. That was the only reason why he was here. And for all he knew, whoever or whatever was responsible for giving him this chance might get peeved if they thought he was misusing it, and yank him back before he had learned anything. Folding the paper, he slipped it into his jacket pocket and then leaned back again, folding his arms, to make a mental list of what he had so far been able to find out.

It was—he twisted his wrist to bring his watch into view—almost mid-day on Saturday, July 6—if it was today's paper—1974. The old man's firm was still in being and, judging by that advert, very much alive and kicking. He was wearing clothes that, if not as cheap as he had first thought—perhaps their very strangeness had made them look cheap—were not of as good quality as those he usually wore. He was worth a little over six quid—not much by '69 standards, no doubt worth even less here in '74—and he appeared to own a car. Anything else? Apart from being somewhere in London, no. Oh, and he—or rather the Howell of "now"—had some connection with a female called Christine Martin. A stranger, he guessed; someone the other Howell had just met, or was intending to meet—else why have her name and address written down like that?

And that was all. Little enough. He'd just have to add to it as time went on. And what was the next move to be? An early lunch, even though he didn't feel all that hungry? He wondered how much a meal in a decent place would cost. A quid, say, back in '69; certainly more than that now. Which would knock quite a hole in his six quid. He had no way of knowing how long it would have to last him. He couldn't afford to waste any of it until he'd found another source of supply. But he had to eat. At home? It all depended where home was now. If he was unmarried, then it was a fair bet he was still living at Ferncroft. But if he'd found himself a wife from somewhere, then home could be anywhere, even maybe here in London, much as he'd always detested towns. There was a third possibility, and that was that he was married and living with his wife at Ferncroft.

If only men wore wedding rings, like women. Then at least he'd have something to go on. As it was, he had to allow for the possibility of his being married. He couldn't risk going anywhere where he might find himself face to face with the stranger who was his wife. Mother would be all right—he ought to be able to persuade her into believing what had happened; she would know he was telling the truth. But a stranger would never believe. So Ferncroft was out until he'd found out more about himself.

But if he was still here in 1974 when night came, he'd have to find himself a bed somewhere. And preferably somewhere where it wouldn't cost him anything. What a hope. He didn't much fancy a bench in a park, but it might have to come to that. Not the one he was sitting on now, but in a real park. London was full of parks filled with trees and benches. Or there was always the embankment. Supposed to be the favourite sleeping-out place for tramps and suchlike. All right so long as it didn't rain or go cold. And in the morning he could always have a wash and shave in a public lavatory.

At which point he pulled himself up, telling himself that letting his thoughts run along those lines was just plain stupid. It was up to him to use his common sense. What he needed was some way in which he could get the use of Howell's money—which was his own money, anyway—without anyone being any the wiser, and without him having to have anything to do with anyone likely to ask questions to which he couldn't supply answers. What he needed was a sort of go-between, a kind of liaison officer between himself and 1974. And who the deuce could he get to do that? There was nobody he could even talk to. But it would have to be a stranger in any case: a stranger both to himself and the Howell of now. Or someone the Howell of now didn't know all that well.

Which reminded him of the name and address on the slip of paper. Taking out the wallet he unfolded the paper again. Bessemer Terrace. S.11. A posh-sounding district. But names don't mean a thing. He wondered again who Christine Martin was, what she was like—the writing, if it was hers, suggested someone fairly young. He had the feeling, a hunch, that Howell hadn't actually met her yet, that she was a friend of a friend or something like that. Knock at her door, watch her expression, see what her reactions were and then play it from there. With a bit of luck she lived with her parents, and with more luck they might turn out to be the sort of people likely to offer a bed for the night. With maybe a meal or two thrown in for good measure. A Trowman on the scrounge. Howell grimaced to himself, wondering what his mother would say if she ever found out. That thought gave way to a small wave of doubt. Was it wise, after all, to get into contact with someone neither he nor the Howell of '74 knew? It wasn't, he supposed, but he had to make a move of some kind, he couldn't risk talking to people who might know Howell, so what else was there? It seemed to him that that slip of paper was his only link between himself and this as yet strange world of 1974.

The woman turned to look at him, the old man opened his eyes again as he came to his feet. He walked back to the main road. Much as he was concerned about husbanding his resources, because he couldn't recall having seen a bus on his way down, because there were none in sight now and anyway, he wouldn't have known where to book to, he put up his hand to a cruising taxi.

It took the driver a few seconds to place Bessemer Terrace, and even then he wasn't sure. "Side street off Milton Road—that the one?"

"I wouldn't know," Howell told him. "I've never been there before."

"We'll find it all right, chum," the driver assured him confidently. "Don't you worry."

3

BESSEMER TERRACE TURNED OUT TO BE much farther
away than Howell had bargained for. The journey took well over
half an hour, and the fare plus only a small tip, took care of one
of his precious pound notes. One down, and with a not very
promising-looking prospect to show.

A forgotten side street of tall grey houses that were poor
relations of those back at Gladwyn Place. The same type, but
of a very different class—stonework rotting, patchy and dis-
coloured; flaking grimy steps; long-neglected paintwork. No elegant porticos, no gleaming black railings, no brass plates. The
round iron bell-pull was almost a museum piece. At least the
middle-aged woman who opened the door looked to be clean
enough for all she was shabbily dressed and tired-looking, a cigarette stuck to her lower lip.

"I'm looking for a Christine Martin," Howell said, a prepared opening, and the woman nodded, stepping aside, telling
him through the cigarette: "Second floor back."

So, by the sound of it just a room, a bed-sitter, and so much
for the hope of a happy family and an invitation to spend the
weekend. He almost turned and went away, would have done
but for the knowledge it had cost him a pound to get here and
anyway, the woman was waiting for him to go in, would think
him queer if he turned and belted away.

He mounted the stairs slowly. Cabbage was part of the overall smell, and some kind of spice—curry, perhaps. And the familiar one of disinfectant; so familiar indeed that just for a few moments he was back at school, chatting to Mick as they climbed the stairs together.

He returned to the present of a landing that was a narrow, badly-lit place of sombre red wallpaper, threadbare carpet and creaking floorboards. Another flight of stairs was a dismal duplicate of the first. And arriving on the second landing, with four doors to choose from, he had to lean over the bannister rail to look down into the hall to remind himself which was the front and which the back of the place.

He rapped on the appropriate door with another small opening speech ready assembled in his mind. It was opened by a woman, which was about all he could tell, for her back was to the light and it was dark in the doorway, making of her little more than a silhouette in some sort of lightish jumper and dark slacks—a thin, narrow-waisted female with no way of telling how old she was, what her face was like. She had a fork in one hand—he could see that much—and a new smell came from the room behind her, that of frying bacon—at this time of day?

She said: "Yes?" shortly and inquiringly, a pleasant enough voice, obviously not recognising him, for which Howell felt relief. But then she came forward a step so that now her face was in the light. A young face, late teens, he estimated; a thin face that was all eyes and mouth, framed by centrally parted straight brown hair. An anonymous sort of face that with those huge dark eyes would have been pretty enough if only there had been more colour to it. And yet she had used make-up; that much was apparent even to his inexperienced eyes; but seemingly had used it to cancel out natural colour instead of enhancing it. Pallid blue eye shadow, white cheeks, pale coral lips.

"You are Christine Martin?" he asked.

And she nodded, asking: "And who do I owe money to now, for God's sake?" And then her voice changed, losing its weary, resigned tone. "Oh, it's you. I didn't know you at first." And then, with another abrupt change of voice: "Don't say you've got something for me already?"

So they had met before after all. Damn. His rehearsed speech was useless now. Nothing for it but to play it as it came, bluff like hades and hope he didn't make a fool or worse of himself.

For a moment he couldn't think of what to say next. It would have to be something she could take any way she pleased. But how to start?

The girl solved the problem for him, demanding with some indignation: "What do you mean, anyway, asking if I was who I am like that? You must have known who I was for you to have come here. Unless you were sloshed last night, enough to have forgotten what I looked like. Were you? Sloshed to the gills and talking and making promises without knowing what you were doing? Though you didn't seem that way to me. Unless you're one of those who take it without it spilling out of their ears. Is that it? And if it is, and you don't remember me from last night, what for Susan's sake are you here now for?"

The small, rapidly delivered little tirade had left her somewhat breathless. A forthright, outspoken person with more than a touch of fieriness, so it seemed to Howell. And for all the near vacancy suggested by her expression, there was a certain light to those large round eyes that suggested here was a girl who wouldn't take easily to being messed about, who liked spades to be called spades and required to be told the truth at any price, no matter how unlikely that truth might seem. A girl, he felt, who could be trusted to keep things to herself. A girl who would listen and at least try to understand. He might be wrong in that assessment of her. For some reason, perhaps a hangover of the Howell of now, who had at least met her once before, he didn't think he was.

"Well?" she demanded, waiting, one hand on slim dark hip, fork in the other, held upright in front of her face like a swordsman in salute.

He needed somebody to confide in. Somebody who might be induced to act as a kind of—not cat's-paw—"agent" would be a better word.

"If I were to tell you the truth," Howell said with all the earnestness of which he was capable, "you wouldn't believe me."

Head held sideways, the girl squinted through the greasy prongs of her fork. "Very impressive. You're saying you weren't plastered last night?"

"I've never been plastered in my life."

"My." She pulled a small face. "I'll believe you. But you had forgotten all about me?"

Howell took a deep breath. "I've never seen you before today. I wasn't at that party last night."

"Well . . ." The fork was lowered, pale eyebrows were lifted.

He leaned against the side of the door, nonchalantly, he hoped. "I told you you wouldn't believe me."

She nodded slowly, eyes searching his face. "So you did, Mr. —" She paused. "Your name's gone. I had it last night. Trueman, is it?"

"Trowman. Howell Trowman. My friends usually call me Howie."

Her eyes narrowed a fraction. "Howie. Do they now." She nodded again. "I remember." Another pause while she studied him, frowning. "You seem very serious about all this. It's really nothing, but you seem all out to make something of it, being all mysterious. All right, so you say it wasn't you last night?"

"It wasn't me."

"This is some kind of gag, of course. I wonder who put you up to it? Never mind, I'll buy it and get it over and done with. Go ahead and tell me all about your twin brother who's the spitting image of you."

"No brothers or sisters," Howell told her.

"So I have to guess again." She gestured with her fork. "No, I don't; life's too short. I give up. So what's the answer?" And when he looked at her in silence, wondering how on earth he could even begin to explain it in such a way the worst she would do would be to laugh in his face: "What are you waiting for now, Howie boy? An invitation? All right." She stepped aside with a flourish. "Come on in. Make yourself at home while

33

you watch me cook what I laughingly call lunch." A small note of bitterness. "Come and see how the other half lives."

He stepped inside. A narrow, musty-curtained window looked out on a blank wall. There was a divan bed against one pale green wall, a dressing table against another. Closing the door behind him with her foot, the girl went across to an alcove, the curtain now drawn aside, that contained a small cooker and and an old-fashioned sink. She turned up the gas under a frying pan, and turned to look back at him over her shoulder. "You wouldn't have any ideas about me inviting you to share my humble meal, would you?"

It was an invitation of sorts, however ungracious. Allied with the frying bacon was another smell. Beans, it seemed like. A few minutes ago, climbing the stairs, he hadn't been particularly hungry. Now, with that smell in his nose, he suddenly was.

"I'd be grateful, if you do have any to spare," he said awkwardly, and wondered if he ought at least offer to pay her something.

"To spare?" Derisive, she didn't bother to turn round. "You must be joking. After last night's sob story telling you how much the welfare job pays and how much my rent is. But I forgot—it wasn't you, was it? All right." She stooped to open the cupboard under the sink. "My last precious rasher. Sunday's breakfast, that was to have been. Now—" She splashed it into the pan. "Share my last crust, that's me. Damn. Old Peabody's sparked out again. Feed him a fivepenny if you've got one, will you, Howie? You'll find him lurking behind that elegant curtain in the corner."

He didn't know what she was talking about. But lifting the curtain revealed a gas meter. Then he understood who Old Peabody was. But why fivepence?

"It's one of the old meters," the girl offered as he hesitated. Which wasn't of any help. Until he had taken the loose change out of his pocket with the idea of finding five pennies, and sight of the silver reminded him again of the change in currency, and that what had once been a shilling was now only five new pennies. He thumbed one into the slot, the first time in his life he had ever put money in a gas meter.

"Ta." The girl turned back to her frying. "Now how about doing something to earn your keep? Set the table. That's that folded contraption over there. Cloth in the left-hand sideboard drawer, knives and forks in the right, plates and suchlike underneath. And while you're working you can give me your story of how come you were and you weren't at the party last night."

Unfolding the card table, Howard put it in the middle of the floor, spent a few minutes—watched with some amusement by the girl—trying to make it steady, then gave up and went over to the sideboard. Her gaze followed him. "Well, Howie? I'm still waiting."

He offered with a rush the first sentence that came to mind. "This morning I was still at school."

"You mean you went back there for something?"

"No." He found a lemon-coloured cloth and opened it out for her approval. She nodded. "And what's going back to school to do with last night, anyway?"

He looked at her steadily. "Will you hear me out without interrupting or laughing? And when I've done, will you at least try to understand"—he tacked on her name, diffident about using it—"Christine?"

"So we've gone all serious again. And I like being called 'Tina.' I told you that last night. All right, Howie, I'll hear you out if that's the way you want it."

So he told her. Surprisingly, the telling took only a few moments, no longer than he would have taken in passing on a smutty story back at school. He told it squatting on his heels in front of the sideboard, looking into the open cupboard at its few crockery contents. He took it to the point where he sat in the garden to collect himself, then rose to his feet and turned to find out how she had taken it.

She wasn't laughing, and that was something. But if he read her face right, she hadn't believed a word of it.

"Well—" She set her hands on her hips. "I've heard some tales in my time, but that one beats the band." Head on one side, she regarded him closely, a change coming to her expression, a small frown creasing her forehead. "But unless

35

you're a very good actor, and I don't think you are, you really believe yourself that that's what's happened."

Behind her the contents of the pan spluttered, and she turned to adjust the gas flame. "Finish setting the table," she ordered, not looking at him. "If it is a gag, I can't see what anyone hopes to get out of it. Unless—" She shook her head. "Nobody in their mind would go to all that trouble just to get out of a promise to try to help a girl get another job."

Howell took plates and assorted pieces of cutlery to the table.

"What promise, Tina?"

"That you'd try to get me a job at the place where you work."

So that was all it had been. Shades of Andy Brett and jobs for the boys. He smiled at the girl as she brought the frying pan over to the table.

"Consider it done," he said lightly. "Nothing easier."

She looked up from dividing the bacon and beans contents of the pan onto the two plates. "You didn't sound all that hopeful about it last night. You just said you'd try."

"It wasn't me," he reminded her.

"No . . ." Frowning again, she took the empty pan to the sink, returned to the table and sat down. "Oh, bread, Howie. In that white bin. You really believe that sometime this morning you were still at school, then suddenly, whamo, it's five years later, you're grown up and here in London?"

He brought a loaf to the table and sat down.

"That's exactly how it was," he told her.

"Has anything like this ever happened to you before?" Busy slicing bread, she avoided looking at him. "Gaps in your memory—you know."

"There's no gap in my memory. One minute I was in my room at school, the next I was in that other room, and there was no gap between the two. If there had been, I'd know. I was hit on the forehead once, playing cricket. It knocked me out— the ball. I was out for about five minutes. But when I came round I knew without having to be told that there was a bit of time I couldn't account for. And that was only a few minutes, not five years. I know what you're thinking, that I've lost five years of memory. I haven't, Tina. Every bit of time is accounted for. I went straight from school to that room in Gladwyn Place without any kind of break. I *know*."

"It's impossible," the girl told her plate, toying with her food instead of eating it.

Howell was making the most of his. He looked at her over his loaded fork. "You're taking it better than I thought you would."

"Probably because I'm stunned. When I've had time to think about it—" She broke off. "It's impossible," she repeated, looking up. "I know it, and you know it. Things like that just don't happen. In books and films, maybe yes. But not in real life. All the same—" Putting down her knife and fork she leaned back.

"All the same, what?"

"Things," she said slowly. "Odd things. About you. You do seem different to what you were last night at the party. Not so—oh"—she gestured vaguely—"stuffy. Not so intense. And when we were introduced, somebody, I forget who, called you 'Howie,' and you said that was a kid's name, or something like that, and your real name was 'Howell.' And yet when you told me your name just now, you said it was 'Howie.'

"And then there was the way you had trouble over the money for the meter. I was watching you. You didn't know at first what I meant by a fivepenny, did you? It's struck me since. If you had come from five years in the past, that would be before we went decimal. You would be used to thinking of a fivepenny as a shilling. I don't think you were acting then. I mean, you didn't even know I was watching.

"And then there was the way you shuffled your feet when you asked if I'd any food to spare. All bashful. Just like an overgrown schoolboy. I don't think that was acting, either. So I'll buy all that. So because something's happened to you to make you think you're only—what?"

"Seventeen. Almost eighteen."

"To make you believe you're only seventeen, you're acting as if that's only how old you really are. I'll buy that, but I don't

37

buy the way you belted out of that room without stopping to find out who it belonged to."

Howell scooped up the last piece of crisp bacon. "The only thing I was worried about was getting out of the place before whoever had been talking to me came back."

"In case they thought you were starkers." She nodded. "That makes sense of a kind. Gladwyn Place . . ." She brooded over the name for a few moments. Then: "Longish, quiet road; large terraced houses, mostly painted white?"

He nodded, pushing his empty plate aside. "Like seaside boarding houses."

"I did a temp there about a year ago," Tina said. "A week, typing for a lawyer. I remember now they were mostly lawyers and suchlike round there. Did your room look like it might have been a lawyer's office?"

He considered. "I don't think so; a bit too posh for that. But there was a case of what looked like reference books. And there was the big desk and the filing cabinet."

Picking up her fork, Tina started to eat the now almost cold food on her plate.

"They don't all look like something out of Dickens," she said. "The one where I worked had his place tarted up like a Mayfair salon. I think your room was a lawyer's office. You know what I think really happened to you, Howie? I think you've been having worries of some kind, and you went along to see this lawyer to try and get things sorted out. Something he told you gave you such a shock you passed out. And then you came round again while he was out getting you a glass of water or something. And you'd lost a slab of your memory. That's what I think must have happened to you."

"I haven't lost any part of my memory," he said patiently. It was only natural she would try to find a rational explanation for what had happened.

"Well, if it's not that, it's something pretty much like it. It's got to be. It can't be the way you say it is. I mean, you've only got to think about it, ask yourself questions. Like, for instance, who or what brought you here, and how was it done?"

"I don't know," he told her equably.

38

His calmness seemed to irritate her. "Of course you don't!" She had started off by seeming to be almost ready to accept his story. Now she was doing her best to break it down. "You say you're just using the body of the you of today, borrowing it for the time being. And what is the you of today doing in the meantime?"

Howell tapped his forehead. "I think he must still be in my head."

"Squashed in one corner," Tina retorted scathingly, "waiting for you to go back where you came from so he can come out again. Give me strength. And what's happening to the body you're supposed to have left back at school? Look, don't you see the whole thing's impossible, Howie. It's just plain ridiculous. The only reason I'm even bothering to argue about it is because I think you're on the level, I think you honestly believe it's happened the way you say it has.

"Look at it another way. You say you've been given the chance of looking at what your future's going to be. So supposing you find it's not so hot, supposing you find you came to the wrong decision way back when you were at school—well, don't you see, you can't go back and unchange it all, because it's all already happened. You see what I'm getting at? What's the use of showing you the future when you can't do anything to change it? It's just pointless.

"Another thing—" She went on quickly, giving him no chance to interrupt. "You come here, you have your look round, and then back you go to—when did you say?—nineteen sixty-nine. And you carry on from there. You leave school, the years roll by, and in due course you go to a party where you meet me. See? Which means that last night, at the party, you must have known what was going to happen today. So why didn't you tell me about it, warn me what to expect?"

That was something that hadn't occurred to him. He would go back to 'sixty-nine and school knowing that on the evening of Friday, July fifth, nineteen seventy-four—that's if today was Saturday—he would go to a party and there meet a girl called Christine Martin and promise to get her a job with his firm. And then the next day . . . What would it be like on the

Saturday—today? A blackout? A sort of gap in his memory? Unless the Howell of now was aware of what was going on— aware but unable to do anything about it. Weird . . .

"Food for thought?" Tina wondered, watching his face.

"I hadn't realised just how queer it all is."

"But you're still sticking with your story?"

"Because I know that that's what's happened."

"I give up." She pushed her empty plate aside and turned to look at the tiny kitchen alcove. "I think it'll run to something to drink. Tea or coffee? Coffee'll be the quickest."

"That'll suit me fine."

She looked back at him from her kitchen recess. "What made you come here to tell me all this, Howie?"

He explained how he had found her name and address in his wallet. "I figured for him to have it written down like that must mean you were someone he didn't know very well, maybe hadn't even met."

"You figured right. But you still haven't told me why you came."

"I needed someone to talk to." There was no point in being anything but frank about it. "Someone I might be able to persuade to help me."

"Help you?" She didn't understand. "What sort of help do you need?"

"I've got to find out what's happened during the last five years. I don't know how long I've got before I'm returned to my own time. I've got to move quickly. But if I try talking to people who know me—friends and relatives—they'll know straight away something's wrong. They'll think I'm sick. I can't afford to waste time with doctors and hospitals."

"And trick cyclists," Tina added. "I see what you mean. But what about your parents? Surely they'd believe you?"

"Mother would, I think. I'm not sure about Dad; that's if he's still alive. But the reason I daren't risk going to Gretton is because for all I know I might be married and living there at home with my people. I couldn't cope with a strange woman."

"If you are married," Tina said wisely, holding the kettle

40

under the tap, "then it'll probably be to someone you already know; she won't be a stranger."

"I don't know any girls," Howell said. "At least not well enough to ask any of them to marry me."

She turned from putting the kettle on the stove.

"I have to admit," she told him, "you've thought of all the trimmings to your story. How did you know what year this is? You said you've talked to nobody but me since you arrived."

He brought the newspaper out of his pocket and unfolded it. "I found this in the litter bin in that garden I told you about."

"Today's?" She came to look. "Yes, it's this morning's."

"I'm going to study it," Howell told her, folding it again. "I can't take it back with me when I go, but I can memorise some of it—racing results, stock exchange prices."

And that, for some reason, seemed to impress her more than anything else he had told her. Staring at him as if seeing him for the first time she lowered herself to her chair again.

She shook her head in slow wonderment. "This is the damnedest, queerest conversation I've ever heard. And here's me, talking as calmly as if it's just the weather we're discussing. More things on heaven and earth—" She pulled a face. "Sorry."

"You're beginning to believe me?" he asked eagerly.

"I didn't say that." The kettle boiled and she went to lift it off. "Football pools," she said inconsequently, pouring. "That's better than horses and share prices. You could really hit the jackpot with football results. Get tonight's paper. No, that's no use; I forgot they're not playing football here now. The Aussie results; those are what they use in the summer. They'll be in tomorrow's paper."

"If I'm still here tomorrow," Howell said. "If only I knew how long I've got. I've been here"—he looked at his watch—"nearly two hours, and all I've been able to find out so far is that the old man's firm is still going strong, and that I run a car. And both those would have been safe bets anyway."

Tina poised a milk jug. "Black or white?"

"White." He watched her pour. "Last night—"

"I know." She brought the two cups of coffee, no saucers, to the table. "You want to know what I can add to your list. Not very much. Last night was the first time I'd clapped eyes on you. The party was in a flat out Knightsbridge way. I'd never been there before; wouldn't die if I never went again. I've got a friend who works in a boutique, and one of her boyfriends—and she gets them by the dozen—invited her to this do, and asked her to bring someone along for a friend of his. I don't usually drift off on blind dates, but I did this time because I'd nothing much on and anyway, it wasn't to be an orgy or anything like that, just a stuffy sort of business do. Which it was. Stuffy, I mean. All people working for the same firm. Chemicals. I forget the name. Anyway, we bumped into each other, you and I, started chatting and that was all. I told you I didn't like being stuck in an office all day, so I worked for a welfare organisation, part time, which meant I got to meet people. The snag was the pay wasn't so hot and I was having a job making ends meet. You said there was a chance you might be able to do something about finding me a travelling job with the firm you worked for—the firm giving the party."

"Trowman Chemicals," Howell said.

"Trowman—the same as your name?" Tina shook her head. "No, that wasn't it. It wasn't two words, just one. You said you'd been with them some time. You weren't all that well in with them—" She broke off. "Trowman . . . Now I come to think I did hear that name mentioned. I thought it rang a bell when you told me your name just now. Trowman. That's it. There were speeches, and somebody stood on a table to propose a toast. Like to the happy couple at a wedding. Only this was to a new product their company had just brought out, and confusion to the enemy. I remember laughing to myself at that— them talking like there was a war on. The enemy being Trowman Chemicals. I've got the other name on the tip of my tongue—"

Howell stared at her. Unless things had changed a great deal during the last few years, unless some other company was now in the running, there was only the one firm likely to call Trowman Chemicals the "enemy."

"Solmex," he said, and Tina nodded brightly.

42

"That's it. They were the ones throwing the party."

But that was impossible. She was confused; she had it the wrong way round.

But she hadn't.

"You said you'd try to get me a job with them," Tina said. "You promised you'd have a word with the manager of the Solmex London office, where you worked."

4

TINA STACKED HER FEW PLATES and cups in the cupboard, hung up the pink-and-white-checked towel on the piece of string that served as a clothesline and came to stand at Howell's side.

"You wouldn't be having me on?" she asked the top of his head.

He looked up at her. "Having you on?"

"When you say your father is the Trowman of Trowman Chemicals."

He was in no mood to offer more protestations that he was telling her the truth. "He's my father," he replied shortly in a take-it-or-leave-it tone.

"It's funny—last night, even though the names were the same, yours and the other firm, I never connected the two. I suppose because I naturally never dreamt you could have anything to do with a big concern like that. But he's your father, and he owns all those factories and things."

"Unless he's dead," Howell said woodenly. "In which case they should belong to me."

"But you're working for Solmex. And by all accounts they and Trowman are at each other's throats."

He leaned forward. "You couldn't be mistaken about last

night, Tina? About who was giving the party; about where I told you I worked?"

She shook her head. "I only had two glasses of booze. I wasn't mistaken."

"You say I said I'd try to get you a job. That means we must have talked together. Did I tell you anything about myself, Tina—anything at all?"

"We chatted all right." She paused while she thought, one finger to her pursed lips. "But not about anything special. This and that. You told me you worked in the London office of Solmex and that you were something to do with exports. And that's about all. You didn't say anything about being connected with the Trowman people, and you didn't say anything about being married. There was one thing, now I come to think. Not anything you said, though. The way the rest of the people there seemed to behave toward you. You weren't one of the boys, you know? You knew all of them, but they didn't seem to want anything to do with you. They were polite enough—'What sort of week have you had, Howell?'— that sort of thing. But nothing very chummy. You left early, before anyone else."

"I've been trying to think of anything that might have made me turn my back on the old man and go to work for his rival." Howell stared at the window. "Even if I'd quarrelled with him, which is something I've never done in my life, I can't see myself feeling bad enough about it to go to Solmex. There's just one thing . . . A takeover. It could be that the decision I took was to go into the firm instead of to university. Then Dad died, and I took charge. But I wasn't up to it, inexperienced, and things came unstuck in a big way. Another firm took us over, leaving the old name as it was. They chucked me out, and Solmex took pity on me. It could easily have been like that. I can't think of anything else it could be. I've got to find out."

Tina put her hand on his shoulder. "Here we go again. We've been through all this. What good will finding out do? What's done is done, and that's it. Don't you see, Howie? You just can't go back to where you came from and change what you did then so that things will happen differently now. They've already happened. Don't you see that?"

He did, and it made sense, but there was another way of looking at it, one that also made sense.

"I must have been brought here for some reason," he said. "There would be no point to it if I can't do anything about it when I get back."

"You haven't been brought here—" she started, and then broke off, taking her hand from his shoulder to gesture resignation. "What's the use. Your mind's made up. We could argue for hours in circles and get nowhere fast. You'll just have to be left to go your own sweet way until something happens to make you find out what really happened to you between last night and now. Me, I'm sticking with my lawyer's office, shock and lost memory idea. What do you propose doing next?"

"Find myself somewhere to stay."

"I was expecting something dramatic like breaking into your office at dead of night to read your personal file. Why do you need somewhere to stay, for Susan's sake?"

"I don't know how long I'll be here," he explained patiently. "Could be for some days. I daren't risk going home to Gretton, and a hotel is out because I've only five pounds in cash."

"That wouldn't be why you came here—looking for a bed?"

He nodded. "Someone to help me, somewhere to stay."

"You've got a nerve. But your home might not be at Gretton now. Had you thought of that? Don't forget you're working here in London. How far is Gretton, anyway?"

"About forty miles from the City centre."

"Not all that far. Have you got a railway season ticket on you?"

Bringing out his wallet he laid it open on the table. "That's almost everything I've got."

"No ticket." She looked up from investigating the few contents. "No driving licence either."

"I've got a car, though." He laid the bunch of keys alongside the wallet, indicating the one attached to the miniature number plate.

She picked it up to examine it. "Well worn. Probably means an oldish car. And where is it now?"

He shrugged. "God knows."

"I remember you saying you walked away from that lawyer's office. So how do you think you got there in the first place? Use your loaf, Howie."

"You think I may have driven there?"

"I'd say it was a dead cert you did. What's the use of owning a car if you don't use it? You drove there, parked it, went into your lawyer's office, had your little brainstorm or whatever, came out and walked away leaving your car still there."

Which made sense. And sounded hopeful. A car would solve the problem of getting about quickly and relatively cheaply. And there might be things in it—papers, letters, stuffed in the glove compartments—that would help fill in some of the gaps of the past five years. Howell came to his feet.

"And how well do you know London?" Tina asked drily, watching him.

"Hardly at all," he admitted.

"So how did you find your way here?"

"By taxi."

"Did you. Does that mean you're rolling in it?"

"I've got the five pounds." He brought out the loose change. "And this."

"Untold wealth. And I suppose you were thinking about taking another taxi back to Gladwyn Place?"

His face told her he was. She went across to the door to take down the short red plastic jacket that hung there.

"It's buses and the Underground for you from now on," she told him, turning, wriggling her arms into the scarlet sleeves.

"Does that mean you're going to help me?" he asked eagerly.

"I wouldn't say that. Let's just say I'm coming with you for the ride. For one thing, you're not fit to be let out on your own in the Smoke. For another, I don't feel like letting you walk out of here, me waving good-bye and never seeing you again. I'd never sleep nights for wondering what it's all about. It's the first bit of excitement that's come my way since the shoulder strap broke on my hot pants in Oxford Street last summer. 'Sixty-nine—" She looked up from fastening her belt. "Did they have hot pants way back then?"

Howell shook his head. "Not that I know of."

"I've seen you looking at me; you've an eye for the girls. If they had hot pants then, you'd have noticed them. Are we ready?"

She didn't bother about checking her face or patting her hair or any of the other nonsense he associated with girls. A quick look round the shabby room and she had the door open and was out on the landing, waiting for him to join her. She led the way downstairs and out into the street, where the sun was still shining and where children played with a rope slung from a lamp-post. It was only a short walk to the bus stop. They sat upstairs in a bus that was going to a place Howell had never heard of. He watched the shops as they slid by. A thread of something—bacon—had jammed itself between two of his back teeth. Freeing it, his tongue found a new and disturbing contour.

Tina, feeling him stiffen in his seat, asked: "What's the matter, Howie?"

He finished a quick tour of inspection before answering. "There's a hole in one of my back teeth." Angry at the failure of the Howell of now to have the cavity seen to—he had always taken great care of his teeth—he did another check. So far as he could tell, the rest of his teeth were all right.

"A hole you didn't know about . . ." Tina sat back. "It's weird. I'm finding myself beginning to believe that you have somehow been brought up out of the past. But that's impossible. How many times have I said that? It's downright, bloody impossible. And yet everything about you fits in with what you say's happened. I give up."

She turned to look through the window. The bus jerked on its way through now busy traffic. When the conductor came for the fare she roused herself in time to stop Howell's hand completing its journey to his pocket.

"You'd better let me pay." She had a purse in the pocket of her shiny, cheap-looking coat. "You may find yourself needing every penny of what little money you've got. No need to thank me; I've always had an eye to the main chance. If you are who you say you are, this could be a good investment on my part. It's not every day I get the chance of doing a millionaire's son a good turn. You can pay me back with interest when you get yourself sorted out."

She turned back to the window. Against the brilliant scarlet of her coat her face looked even more colorless. And across the aisle another girl had the same sort of ivory and pallid pink make-up. A new look for faces, Howell supposed. Otherwise there was very little difference between the girls of now and those of 'sixty-nine. Brief skirts were still very much in evidence on the crowded pavements, but from time to time he spotted touches of the exotic—floppy wide-brimmed hats and sweeping cloaks; flared trousers and flamboyant lace shawls.

The bus halted at traffic lights. The jerk brought his companion out of another small reverie.

"Howie—the way you spoke earlier—if anything did happen to your father, there's only you for it." And to make sure he understood: "To take over the firm, I mean. Isn't there anyone else in the running? I know you said you hadn't any brothers or sisters, but what about cousins and uncles and things? Don't get me wrong. I'm not being curious just for the sake of it. It just struck me that what might have happened is that your father died, but instead of you taking his place, someone else did, and you were that peeved you went to work for another firm. Could it have been like that?"

It was a possibility that had occurred to him, but one that was too remote to merit serious consideration.

"I've no relatives at all," he explained. "There's Uncle Wilf, but he isn't really my uncle—that's just a name that's stuck since I was a kid. He and Aunt Meg are the nicest people under the sun. But there's no chance of him ever taking over the firm. He's just not made for it. Not capable of dealing with crises. There was one once. He and Dad started up the business from nothing, back in nineteen thirty-six. Things were going nicely until the war came along and put the kibosh on it. Dad said from the start they'd weather it all right, but Uncle Wilf threw a panic and wanted out. He's too gentle—

49

that's his only fault. If you can call it a fault. You've got to be hard where business is concerned, not get rattled at anything. Anyway, Dad bought him out, and then when the war was over, took him back, first as works' manager, then general manager. Which is what he still is today." Howell remembered. "Or was five years ago. But apart from Uncle Wilf not being suitable, Dad's always had his heart set on me taking over from him."

"He sounds nice, your Uncle Wilf," Tina said. "If you don't feel like going home, why not go to him, tell him what's happened to you?"

He nodded. "I had thought about it. They'd listen right enough, but knowing them and the way they worry, as soon as they got the chance they'd be on the phone to the nearest doctor. And I have the feeling I can't afford to waste time with doctors."

The bus shuddered to another halt. Tina glanced out of the window and came to her feet. "This will do us nicely."

He followed her down the stairs and into the street. Taking hold of his arm she hurried him across the street, weaving her way expertly through the busy traffic. He had no time to notice the name over the entrance to an Underground station. Tina bought tickets from a row of machines. A scarlet train rumbled in as they reached the platform. Standing in the packed coach, grasping a leather strap, he swayed and lurched through his first ever journey on the London Underground.

It was a relief to emerge into the open again. Another busy road to cross, Tina's hand in his; another wait for another bus, and then another journey, only short and through mainly residential parts. A few minutes' walk and they were there.

Because they had approached Gladwyn Place from the opposite direction he didn't recognise it at first, one quiet, car-lined street of colour-washed seaside boarding houses looking much like another. Then Tina said: "Before we start looking for where you left your car, how about having a go at trying to remember which door you came out of?"

Then he recognised the place. "On the other side. About halfway along. I think."

They crossed over, no passing traffic to worry about now. Every door looked the same as the next. They walked slowly along. After a while he stopped, turning to look back. "It could have been any one of these."

They retraced their steps, Tina reading brass plates at random. "Advertising Agency, lawyer, lawyer, Oxfam, dentist, Modelling Agency, more lawyers—I told you that's what they mostly were—I worked down at the far end—sewing machines, Private Enquiry Agent, doctor—could it have been a doctor's surgery, Howie?"

Even though he had only seen the room briefly, he was able to picture it vividly, without having to close his eyes. It had certainly borne no resemblance to a doctor's surgery.

He shook his head. "I think you were right when you said the most likely thing was a solicitor's office. I don't see that there's anything else it could have been."

"What about the private detective?" she mused, but shook her head. "We'd only be guessing, anyway. Let's look for your car, Howie. What's the number again?" He took the bunch of keys out for her to see.

She recited the registration number aloud. "TYD four-six-three E. Got it. We'll start at the bottom of the street and work up. I'll take this side, you the other. Whoever spots it, sings out."

But they worked their way from one end of the street to the other without finding the car. Standing on the corner, Howell raised his shoulders and spread his hands in a pantomime that was intended to say it looked like he couldn't have driven there after all. But the girl wasn't ready to give up. She motioned for him to round the corner and check the vehicles in the right-angle road while she did the same in the other direction.

He made his way slowly along until he reached a main thoroughfare with no further parking spaces, turned, crossed over and came back down the other side, looked up at one point and there was Tina in the distance, waving and beckoning.

He hurried to join her. She led him to where a car—his car, that he had never seen before—was parked behind a television rental van. He eyed it with some dismay—a small black saloon that had patently seen better days. Old—it would have been old five years ago—but in reasonable shape.

"I did warn you that from the way the key was worn, the car would probably be oldish," Tina offered, reading his expression.

"Oldish . . ." He tried the doors; they were both locked. "It's only fit for scrap." But that was an exaggeration, born of his disappointment. After the lines of elegant gleaming limousines in Gladwyn Place, this. He checked the number to make sure it was the right car. It was. He tried the small key. It opened the door and fitted the ignition. Sliding into the driving seat he investigated the glove compartments. Tina leaned over his shoulder, breathing heavily in his ear, the better to see what he was doing.

The first compartment contained only a bunch of oily rags and a dirty pair of washleather gloves. The second had an envelope and a road map of London and the Southern Counties to offer. He seized eagerly on the envelope. It contained a receipted dry cleaning bill made out to Howell Trowman Esq. Tina read out the address aloud. "Rear Sixteen, The Barony, Pickham, S.E. Fifteen. Sounds very posh. So now you know where you live. Or where you're lodging." She glanced sideways into his face. "Does it ring any bells?"

He shook his head. "I've never even heard of Pickham before."

"I have. I think." She mused for a few moments, white teeth nibbling on pale lower lip. "Yes, I have. I used to share digs with a girl called Oona, who wore smocks and wooden beads and had an aunt who lived in Pickham. She took me to meet her once. What do I remember of the place? Biggish sort of houses. Faded grandeur. Like it had once been a snob residential district. Your address sounds like it might be a back-street mews of some kind. I think I could find my way there without getting us lost."

Howell eased himself out of the car so that she could climb in without having to walk round to the opposite door. And having slid into the seat she hugged herself happily, a child on an outing, enjoying every minute, inviting him to join in her pleasure. "Isn't this exciting, Howie? Like playing at detectives. Or going on a treasure hunt."

But then her smile went, her display of pleasure faded as quickly as it had come. A grown-up again—as near a grown-up as she could ever be with her small, childish face—she became serious and concerned.

"But it might not turn out to be so much fun for you when you do find your way back home." She leaned forward to look in the direction of the entrance to Gladwyn Place. "Whatever it was you found out in that room of yours, it must have been pretty awful to have done this to you."

5

THE DRIVING SEAT FELT STRANGE and familiar at the same time. He experimented with the gear lever, trying to accustom himself to its feel. It was stiff; perhaps the car had been recently serviced. But the driving wheel, when he tested that, was loose, with several unsafe inches of play. He switched on the engine—healthy enough by the sound—but instead of moving off he leaned back, hands resting on the wheel.

Now that it seemed he was on the verge of discovery it had suddenly become important that Tina believe—or at least make some real effort to believe—the truth of his story of having come from the past. Until she did—and hopefully there had been those times when she had given the appearance of being halfway to believing—there would always be the uncomfortable feeling that she was humouring instead of helping him, that at the first chance she would drag others in—not for her own sake but to help him regain the memory she was so sure he had lost. He could well understand her reluctance to accept the truth. In her place he would be the same. He needed proof of some kind, something he could set in front of her that could only be explained away by his story being true. Proof . . .

He stared through the windscreen, thinking back to the start of it all. Back to his room at school, sitting down there waiting for Mother and Dad to arrive, trying to decide what he was going to tell them. He pictured the scene, still vivid in his mind. He pictured the room as it had started to change about him. Like a transformation scene at the theatre . . .

The girl, putting the wrong construction upon his silence and distant expression, intruded her sympathy and understanding.

"You're afraid now of what you might find when we get there, Howie?"

Afraid . . . He returned to the present. Analysing his feelings, he found no fear of any kind there. No sensation of anything but curiosity. In some odd way he felt himself completely dissociated from the reality of the present, not part of the time in which he was now existing, only a visitor, an observer who would soon be returning to his own time. Armed with the knowledge that would enable him to come to the right decision back in nineteen sixty-nine.

He lowered his gaze from windscreen to wheel. And the sight of his hands resting there brought back part of a picture he had forgotten. Something surely that she would have to accept as proof of his story.

In his haste to tell it to her the words came tumbling out, almost incoherently.

"On the telly, Tina, or at the flicks. One scene melting into another. You know what I mean. So that just for a bit you can see part of each, one laid on top of the other."

She frowned perplexity at him. "Come again?"

He forced himself to speak more slowly. "The way it was when I came here. There I was, like I told you, in my room at school. I must have looked down at my hand; I'd forgotten till now. There it was, resting on the wooden arm of my chair. And then the switch came, and there was my hand on the wide leather arm of that chair in the other room. Only it wasn't two separate pictures. They overlapped. Just for an instant I could see the arms of both chairs. You see what that means? There was no gap because they did overlap. And if there wasn't any gap, then I just couldn't have lost a chunk of my memory. See?"

She was unconvinced. "You couldn't have invented that—not intentionally, I mean—to back up a story that your subconscious or whatever you call it has made up?"

He shook his head firmly, in no way put out by her suggestion. "I didn't invent it. I can see it as clearly now as when it happened."

"I give up." The girl moved her thin shoulders under the scarlet plastic. "It's beyond me. You read all sorts of things in books and the papers . . . I suppose almost anything's possible." She turned back to the front. "Straight ahead, Howie, and left at the top."

He glanced at the dashboard clock as he let in the clutch. Almost half past one. He had been here for only a little over a couple of hours and it felt like a lifetime. A lifetime in which he had been able to find out very little about himself. But now he did at least know where he lived—or rather where the Howell of now was living or lodging. Which meant a roof over his head and a bed for the night. And the chance of going through his papers and things with every hope of being able to add to his store of information. That's assuming he was living alone at Rear 16, The Barony, and not sharing the place with someone else. A man, maybe. Even worse, a wife. Finding out what the set-up there was could be tricky.

He turned left into the stream of traffic on the main road, driving slowly, cautiously, while he gradually came to get the feel of the car, refusing the temptation to put his foot down when the traffic thinned, leaving the road ahead clear. Concentrating upon his driving, he had no idea which direction they were taking. At his side Tina issued instructions, confidently at first, then, as they entered a maze of side streets, with some hesitation, doubtful now at each corner they came to.

But her sense of direction was good. She recognised a church, a gaunt ugly building. The Barony was the third turning on the right past the church, a sweeping, tree-lined curve of large, three-storeyed terraced houses. And behind them, reached by a narrow archway only wide enough to take one vehicle at a time, was the Rear Barony. Enclosed, but for the entrance, a long courtyard rather than a mews or a road, cobbled, with a red-brick wall along one side and a row of garages along the other. From between each pair of white-painted double doors iron stairways led up to the flats above. There were two large tubs filled with scarlet geraniums. Some kind of creeping plant with pale blue flowers trailed from a balcony rail.

Instead of turning in through the arched entrance, Howell drove a little way past before stopping, switching off the engine and turning to look back over his shoulder.

After a few minutes Tina nudged him impatiently with her elbow. "Don't you want to see what sort of pad you've got? Or is it you think you recognise the place?"

He shook his head. "I've never been here before."

"Well?" She nudged him again. And then, suddenly understanding his reluctance: "Windy, is that it? Still thinking you might be married and the little woman will be waiting for you in there? I shouldn't worry; if you ask me, I don't think for one minute you are married. If you were, that dry cleaning bill would have been made out to Mrs. Trowman, not you. Wives usually look after that sort of thing. Still, if you want me to go and spy out the land, just say the word."

"If you would," he said thankfully.

"Muggins." She climbed out of the car. "Number sixteen, was it? And what do I do if a blond dilly opens the door—tell her I've brought her old man home, or say I've come to read the meter?"

Watching her walk away, absently noting the pleasant sway of her narrow hips, Howell wondered what he would do if he did have a wife waiting for him at home. One thing was for sure, and that was that he mustn't actually meet her, for that would mean even more time being wasted on explanations that wouldn't be believed anyway. On the other hand it would be missing a golden opportunity if he weren't to at least take a look at the girl he had picked to be his wife. And if he didn't much care for what he saw? Impossible to go back and change things, according to Tina, and he had to admit that by all the rules of common sense she had to be right. Once something has happened, you can't go back and make it not happen. And so back to the old puzzle of why had he been brought here if there was nothing he could do about it.

Tina was away only a few minutes. She came back, high heels tapping briskly, her coat off and carried slung over her shoulder, one side of her face covered by a soft curtain of brown hair. He climbed out of the car to meet her.

"All clear." She tossed her coat on to the back seat. "At least nobody came to the door. But she could have been taking a bath or something. Shall we go and find out?"

"Thanks," he said. She took his arm as they made towards the entrance. "Don't mention it. Only too glad to oblige. What do I do—keep on helping you until you either get your memory back or else just vanish in a puff of smoke? But according to you, what I suppose will happen is all at once I'll find myself talking to a stranger I've only met once before at an office party."

They turned into the courtyard.

"Quiet," Tina observed unnecessarily. "Like the grave. No sounds at all and not a soul in sight. All right if you like that sort of thing. Not too pricey, I wouldn't think, being so far out. Yours is second from the end. I would say this is where the chauffeurs belonging to the big houses used to live. Here we are."

The skeletal metal staircase led up from alongside a garage that was much larger than Howell had first thought, certainly wide enough to take two cars. He tried the white doors, finding them locked. About to follow the girl up the stairs he changed his mind, taking the keys from his pocket to see if one of them fitted the lock.

One of them did. The doors rolled back smoothly. A car stood to one side the garage, only small, but obviously fairly new and of a make that was strange to him, probably Continental. While he stood looking at it, Tina pattered back down the stairs to find what was keeping him.

"You either run two cars," she reasoned, "or else you share your flat with someone. Or else you just share your garage space."

"It's not mine, otherwise I'd have another ignition key. In any case—"

He had been about to say that judging from the quality of the clothes he was wearing and the kind of car he knew belonged to him, it was most unlikely he could afford to run two cars.

"In any case what?" Tina asked.

"Nothing," he grunted, trying the car doors. All locked, there was no way of finding out if the vehicle contained anything that might offer a guide to its ownership. But so far as he could tell, peering in through the window, both the glove compartments were empty anyway.

Tina, impatient again, tugged at his arm. "Come on, Howie, I can't wait to see what sort of place you've got."

He followed her up the short flight of iron steps to an enclosed, gloomy landing with walls on either side, blank but for two small frosted-glass windows on the left and a door on the right. The front door of the flat. His front door. He fitted the last key of the three into the lock. It turned easily enough, clearly the right one, but still the door refused to budge. Until, turning the key in the lock again to make sure it had caught, he found the door opened outwards, awkward in the confined space of the narrow landing, squashing him against the wall.

But it had been made to open that way because the hall into which it led was even more confined, long and narrow, with two doors in the wall facing him, badly, perhaps makeshift planned.

He left it to the girl to lead the way on a tour of exploration. She started with the left-hand of the two doors. A long kitchen was lighted from above by mesh-covered skylights let into the ceiling. It contained a small sink, a gas cooker and the bare essentials of furniture. A door at the far end led to a bathroom. "Empty," Tina discovered with mock disappointment.

A door on the right opened on to another long narrow room —were all the rooms to be of the same awkward shape? A combined lounge and dining room judging by the table against one wall and the arrangement of two easy chairs and well-worn settee against the other. Shabby, that was Howell's impression. Adequately furnished was about the best one could say about it. Nothing new and the walls in need of new paper. Almost depressing, but that might be because, like the kitchen, the living quarters were also lighted from above—prison-like skylights.

Two more doors led to bedrooms, and that was it. Howell waited by the open door of the first while his companion, thoroughly enjoying herself, investigated the room—at least a proper window here, overlooking the courtyard; the single bed made up, not all that neatly, but clean enough. And then he waited at the door of the second bedroom, a duplicate of the first, even to the made-up single bed. And seeing it, Tina turned to look at him with questioning brows.

"Not a wife," he said. "Not two separate rooms."

"Unless you've quarrelled and aren't on speaking terms." And at his sudden expression of dismay: "Stupid. I didn't mean that. I'd say by the set-up you're sharing with another man. We'll soon find out."

She opened the door of the small wardrobe. "See?" And stepped aside so that he could view the contents: a suit on a hanger, a raincoat, flannels. "Are these your things or the lodger's?"

"How should I know?" He went to stand at her side. A musty smell came from the wardrobe. Tina lifted out the grey jacket of the suit. "Here, take yours off, Howie, and try this on for size."

But there was no need for that. Slipping it off the hanger she found the small cloth tab attached to one sleeve.

"It's just been cleaned, see? Here's your name: Trowman. This must be what that bill was for. These are your togs. Let's go see what we can find out about who's living with you."

The wardrobe in the other bedroom was larger and held many more clothes. Clothes that even to Howell's inexperienced eye were of better quality and cut than those that apparently belonged to him. Tina had no qualms about thrusting her hand into every pocket she could find. But all that three suits, two sports jackets and several pairs of flannels had to offer was a nail file in a leather case.

While Howell, eager to find out who he shared the flat with but oddly reluctant to touch anything belonging to that some-one, watched from the doorway, she went across to the small dressing table by the window. Apart from two small cut glass bowls the top was bare, and before opening any of the drawers she stooped, inspected and then ran the tip of one finger across the expanse of polished wood, holding it up for him to see the black oval of the dust it had collected.

"Someone's not been doing their housework." A casual remark offered for what it was worth. But then, after opening the top drawer she paused and turned to look at him again. "The one in your room was clean, else I'd have noticed. Which could mean that whoever uses this room, hasn't used it in some time. There's not that much dirt kicking about in this part of the world, and the window's closed anyway. I'd say it's taken a few weeks for dust to settle as thick as this. How's that for a clever bit of detective work?"

He came to see for himself how thick the dust layer was.

"Perhaps we each take care of our own room, and he's not as keen on dusting as I am."

"That's not it, Howie." She invited him to inspect the contents of the open drawer: neatly folded shirts; socks in tidy bundles; handkerchiefs, shorts and vests looking to be fresh from the laundry. "Anyone who keeps his clothes as tidy as this wouldn't let dust collect. I'll stick with my first guess. This room hasn't been used for some time."

There were three drawers in the dressing table. The middle one was filled with bed linen; the bottom one was empty. Tina turned to survey the rest of the room. "Any place else where anything might be kept?" Only a small bedside cupboard with a ring-stained top. And inside, nothing but impersonal odds and ends—a brush and comb, a tin of adhesive plasters, a writing pad and ball-point pen.

She straightened, frowning, hands on hips. "That's it, Howie. That's everything. And if you ask me, it's bloody odd."

"What is?" Howell wanted to know, still standing by the dressing table.

"Well, you can see for yourself. Nothing personal in the place. No old letters or bills or anything with a name on. I mean, you think—there's always personal stuff kicking round in the place where you live. No matter how neat you are, you can't stop it accumulating. But here, nothing. It's not natural. It's almost as if somebody had been through the place removing anything that would help you find out who's been living here with you. Let's take a look in the big room to see if there's anything there. I have a hunch there won't be."

He followed her back into the long lounge cum dining room where the only piece of furniture worth investigating was the rather battered, dark-wood sideboard with its pair of cupboards and two narrow drawers.

All it contained were the things sideboards usually contain—cutlery and a not overclean tablecloth in the drawers, an assortment of crockery and other various domestic odds and ends in the cupboards.

Tina closed the doors with her knee and looked back over her shoulder at Howell. "If you ask me, I'd say someone's gone through the place with a toothcomb."

He shook his head. "I think you're trying to make a mystery out of nothing."

"I don't think I am. I've shared digs with quite a few different kinds of people in my time. All girls—don't get the wrong idea. I know what I'm talking about. And you can't deny there's nothing in this place that could give the slightest clue as to who's been living here with you. You can't argue about that."

He couldn't, but he had found a possible explanation for the absence of personal trivia. "He's gone away on holiday, taking all his private stuff with him."

"And left his car behind. That's not likely, now is it?" Her expression changed. "Although, come to think, I don't remember seeing any suitcases in his room. Everybody owns at least one case."

She went back in the bedroom. "Where does one usually stow cases? On top of the wardrobe." But there was nothing there. "Under the bed, then." On hands and knees she reached under the bed to drag out a suitcase. Dusty, covered quite thickly with dust and fluff—no initials, no old labels, unlocked and empty. She pushed it back out of sight again. "At least that puts paid to your away on holiday theory."

"He could have owned more than the one case."

"So he could." On her feet again she dusted her hands together with a grimace of distaste. "I'll need a bath after this

62

lot. But that's a good case. Leather. Must have cost plenty. I'm guessing it's the only one he's got. So where is he now, how long has he been away, and why did he, or someone else, take great care to remove everything that might tell strangers like us who he was? Because they have, you know. I don't care what you say."

Leaving her with her imagined mystery—clearly enjoying herself—Howell returned to the other bedroom. His bedroom, his bed, where he must have slept at night. Where the Howell of now must have slept, rather. This time it was the girl's turn to watch as a room was explored. Not much neatness about the contents of the dressing table drawers. But then he had never won any medals for tidiness at school. That was one thing that hadn't changed. Everything in a sort of ordered jumble —handkerchiefs, clean and used; brush and comb and jar of hair cream—his shaving gear would be in the bathroom—ties and shirts and socks.

And in the second drawer, under a pile of cellular vests, he came across another link with the past. There had been his wallet, now here was something else—a scarf in the school colours of narrow emerald and gold stripes on black; not the one Aunt Meg had knitted and which, after washing, had stretched and stretched until it was three times the original length, but one of the several shop ones that had come his way as Christmas or birthday presents. Just who had given him this one he didn't know, but it was nice to think it had weathered the last five years and was still going strong.

And in the same drawer was a pile of bills, some receipted, some seemingly unpaid. Mostly for petrol and oil and servicing, he saw. His driving licence was there too, and a car insurance policy. All with his name and this address on them.

"The man you're living with has a car," Tina said over his shoulder. "So he'd have bills and things like those, wouldn't he? And he'd have them tucked away somewhere like you have. Only they're not there now."

The bottom drawer was locked.

"D'you have the key?" she wanted to know.

"You know damn' well I haven't," he grunted shortly, needled by her persistence that something mysterious was going on.

"Keep your hair on. So if you don't have it on you, it's probably in here somewhere. Where are you likely to have hidden it? Everyone has a pet place for hiding keys."

"I haven't. I've never had to hide keys."

"You're lucky. You wait till you start sharing digs." Crouching at his side she tried the drawer for herself. "Locked, all right. We could force it, Howie."

"I suppose so." He didn't sound too enamoured of the idea.

"It wouldn't do all that much damage, and anyway, it is your dressing table. I mean, that's why you're here, isn't it, to find out what you can about yourself? You haven't had much luck so far. This might change it. For you to have this drawer locked up probably means there's something special inside." She stood up. "I'll see what I can find in the kitchen."

She came back with an ordinary, yellow-handled table knife and a can-opener. "This is the best I can find. You ever done this sort of thing before?"

He took the things from her without replying. She crouched at his side again. The blade of the knife fitted easily enough into the crack over the lock, but bent the moment he started to apply pressure. The pointed blade of the opener was much stouter. Wood splintered whitely. Then, by pressing down on the lock he was able to work the drawer out.

All it contained was a brief case, an ordinary brown leather brief case, bulging, quite heavy when he lifted it, certainly very far from empty. And it was unlocked. Tina's warm excited face against his, they peered inside.

At neat rows of bundles of bank notes.

6

TINA THOUGHT THEY OUGHT TO FIND OUT just how much money the brief case contained. "Not just idle curiosity, Howie. You never know, the amount might be important."

Just an excuse to get her hands on it, Howell thought; to play with it, like this was a game of Monopoly. But he could have been wrong, for she only bothered to count seven or eight bundles at random. "I think we can take it as read there's a hundred in each. All in fives and tens, no singles, and all old notes. You want to know how much there is?"

"Not particularly," he told her from his seat on the settee.

"You should, it's your bread. At least I suppose it's yours. Fifteen thousand, three hundred. I thought it would be more than that." She was vaguely disappointed. "It looked more, all spread out. Still—" She started feeding the slim bundles back into the brief case. "Fifteen thousand's not to be sneezed at. Bread in anyone's language. And you've no idea what it's in aid of, Howie?"

"Of course I haven't."

The shortness of his tone made her look up. "I know. Instead of a nice normal sort of future you've landed smack in the middle of dirty work at the crossroads. You must admit now there's something fishy going on. Ordinary folk don't keep this sort of money kicking about the house. Unless they're running a one-man business and they're out to evade tax. Which you're not. In business on your own account, I mean. Unless you've got a side-line you didn't tell me about last night. And don't try telling me now you've been saving up for your holidays."

"It can't be mine," he said flatly.

She resumed packing the money away. "And what makes you so sure?"

"If I'd that much money I'd be wearing better clothes than these and driving a damn' sight better car."

She considered the point without interrupting her work. "Maybe you haven't had it long enough to start in spending it. How about starting now?"

"What do you mean?"

She waved one of the bundles at him. "You could start by treating me to a slip-up dinner to make up for pinching my Sunday rasher."

One of the reasons why he had come here was to see if the Howell of now had any money lying round. A few odd pounds tucked away in a drawer would have been all right. But this . . .

"It's not mine," he said.

It was her turn to speak sharply. "The you of then and the you of now, what difference does it make, you're both the same person. So you say, anyway."

"It's not his either."

"Now how can you know that unless your memory's starting to come back? Is it?"

His temper flared. "How many more times do I have to tell you—" he started angrily, and then bit the rest of it off. Nothing to be gained by starting a shouting match.

"I'm sorry, Howie." She snapped the brief case shut. "It must seem like I'm harping on lost memories. I'll put this back where I found it." She looked up from closing the abused drawer. "I bet the bloke you share these digs with knows something about this. And it might help you get sorted out if we were to find out who he is. I mean, he might be someone you already know. What do we do—have a talk with some of the neighbours?"

66

He thought about it. "They must all know me."

"I know that. It would have to be muggins again. I could figure out some excuse or other for knocking on their door and asking questions."

On second thought it didn't seem such a good idea. "It might attract attention." No, that didn't sound right. He tried again. "If there is something fishy going on, a stranger asking questions about who lives here might not be too clever."

"You could be right at that." Tina nodded. "If there is something underhand about that money, and I'm saying it's more than likely, then the quieter things are for the other you, the better he'll like it." She pulled one of her small nose-wrinkling faces. "Hark at me—'the other you.' I'm getting as bad as you. Maybe we ought to call him Howell and you Howie so's we can tell the two of you apart. All right"—at his expression—"I'm not trying to be sarcastic or anything. So where do we go from here?"

"I could go home," he said slowly, a new idea occurring to him.

The girl was surprised. "I thought that was off. I thought you were dead against going home for fear you have a wife tucked away there. What's made you change your mind?"

"Something I hadn't thought of before." A plan had already taken shape in his mind. "Not right now, not in daylight. Tonight, when it's dark. I know how to get in the house without anyone knowing. They wouldn't even know I'd been. Dad uses one room as an office. The small lounge. If he's—" He changed his mind about using the word "dead." "If he's not there any more, then it'll have become my room. I won't have altered anything. All the papers and stuff will be there. And his diary. He used to keep a diary; I'll have done the same. It'll all be written down: everything that's happened over the last five years. Everything."

"You can't be sure." Tina was doubtful. " 'Home' being Gretton?"

He nodded excitedly. "I should have thought of this before. The house is called Ferncroft. It's the biggest for miles. Not counting Ferncroft Hall, but that's where the firm has its head office, nobody actually lives there."

She nodded in the direction of the dressing table. "And what about that little lot? I doubt whether you'll find any mention in your diary about where that came from."

He thought differently. "If the money's his, there'll be some mention of it somewhere."

She sniffed. "You hope." And looked at her watch. "Not till dark, and it's only quarter to three now. How long will it take to get there?"

He wasn't sure about that, not knowing exactly where he was. "Something over an hour," he guessed. "If we start about half past eight it should be dark by the time we get there."

"And you want I should stick round?"

For a moment, taking it for granted she would be coming with him, he didn't get her meaning. Then: "Of course I do."

"Only you won't need my help to break into your own home."

"I'd be lost without you," he said so warmly that he surprised himself. And the girl too, by the way she raised her brows.

The moment passed. "Just so long as we know where we are," she said. "Right. I don't suppose you've any bright ideas about taking me out on the town, which means I'd better scout round the kitchen and see what I can find. Something to keep us going quite a while, I imagine. That's assuming you intend driving back here to London once you're through with your housebreaking. It's going to be very late before we get back."

At the door she paused to add: "At least it's Sunday tomorrow. I don't have to turn in to work. Neither will you." She paused again at another thought. "But what will you do when Monday morning comes round? I don't suppose you even know where your place of work is, do you?"

"I don't really think it matters," he replied enigmatically.

She took his meaning. "You reckon you won't be here when Monday comes round?"

"Not if I manage to fill in the five-year gap tonight, and there's no reason why I shouldn't."

"Weirdo," Tina said, and, shaking her head, went off to the

kitchen. After a few minutes, for something to do he followed her. She was on her way back; they met in the long lounge. She had a piece of paper in her hand.

"Pinned up inside the cupboard." She held it up for him to see. "Missed by whoever went over the place. A shopping list, I would think."

"Sugar, matches, soap" was written in pencil, and he thought she was wondering if he could identify the writing. But that wasn't it. She turned the paper round so that now he could see the list had been scrawled on the back of an envelope. And on the front was the address: *Rear 16, The Barony. Pickham, S.E.15.* This address. And the name above: *Mr. Martin Debroy.*

"You know him?" Tina asked, watching his face.

He nodded. "I'll say. We were at school together. We still are, come to that. Mick, we call him. God knows why. We were talking together only a few minutes before I came here." He remembered something of that particular conversation. "Of course, he told me he'd got himself a job with Solmex. He was joking about it, pretending to be worried if that would mean we wouldn't have to have anything more to do with each other. And if I work for Solmex as well, it's natural enough we should share the same lodgings."

"Debroy—" Tina frowned. "I seem to have heard that name somewhere before."

"Probably at the party last night. I must have mentioned him to you."

"Perhaps." But the explanation didn't seem to satisfy her.

"He'll be all right," Howell said. "If I can find him he'll believe me when I tell him all about this; he'll help me all right."

Tina, still frowning into space, didn't hear him.

"Debroy. Not a common sort of name. Maybe that's why it's stuck in my mind. Martin Debroy." She nodded at its sound. "Rings a bell right enough. Damn." She shook her head, annoyed with herself—"It'll come"—and returned to the problem in hand, the problem of an almost empty larder. She listed its contents. "Half a not very fresh loaf, a can of sardines —yuk, a small piece of mousetrap—a can of evap milk and something unidentifiable in a paper bag. Looks like neither you nor your friend were in the habit of eating at home. I think I'd better go shopping. The thing is, my credit won't be good at any of the local shops."

Which was as good a way as any of asking for money. Howell, still happy at the discovery of Mick being his stable companion, reached for his wallet, then changed his mind, going instead back into his bedroom to crouch by the dressing table, open the bottom drawer, open the brief case and take out one of the bundles.

If this was the Howell of today's money, then taking some was all right, because nobody can rightly be said to rob himself. And if it wasn't Howell's, then it must be Mick's, and that was all right too, for Mick would never say no to a loan under such circumstances.

A loan . . . Something, then, on which to write his I.O.U. Straightening, he handed Tina, waiting in the doorway, two of the five-pound notes, motioning for her to give him the envelope. He had to go into the other bedroom, Mick's room and so now a friendly room, for the ball-point pen. He wrote: "I.O.U. ONE HUNDRED POUNDS" in block letters, signed his name firmly underneath and, after a moment of thought, added the date, his date: "June 2, 1969," and slipped it into the case before closing it.

Tina giggled over his shoulder. "That'll shake him when he reads it. Although he'll probably think it's a gag. You've no idea where he could have got to, Howie? Do you know where his home—"

Somebody knocked at the front door.

She started forward automatically, then stopped, turning to look at Howell. He shook his head at her, laid his finger on his lips and went over to the window to stand with his back to the wall while he peered cautiously out without disturbing the net curtain. A large black saloon was parked just outside.

"Had I better go and see who it is?" Tina whispered urgently, her lips close to his ear. "It might be somebody who knows your friend and can tell you where he is. I needn't say anything about you being here."

70

"And how do you explain who you are and why you are here on your own?" he whispered back, and she pulled one of her gamine faces at him. And then pressed closer against his side, a very pleasant contact, as the knocking came again, three sharp impatient raps. And a few moments later the obvious originator of the knocks appeared down in the courtyard—a hatless, grey-haired elderly man wearing a loose grey coat and managing to look vaguely professional. He turned to look up at the windows, stood for a moment in apparent indecision and then, instead of getting into the car, walked a short distance down the yard and then climbed the stairway leading up to one of the other flats.

"Anyone you know?" the girl asked then.

Howell shook his head. "Never seen him before."

She eyed the car. "Posh job. Not that he was all that well-dressed himself. Lawyer, maybe." And changed her mind. "No, they always wear hats." And at his grin: "Well, they do, or hadn't you noticed?"

The grey-haired man reappeared down below, no longer alone. His companion was also bare-headed, and jacketless, wearing a chunky, once-white pullover that was high in the neck and covered his stocky body almost as far as his knees. Youngish, in his thirties, Howell guessed, with features to match the pullover—chunky, pleasant-ugly, with an almost boxer's nose, heavily pouting lower lip, comedian-arched black bushy brows and a vigorous mass of thick curly black hair with a very pronounced widow's peak.

"What about him?" Tina whispered, even though ordinary speech wouldn't have carried outside the room. Howell shook his head. "Another stranger."

The two men down below spoke together, the elderly man turning at one stage to point in the direction of the arched entrance to the courtyard.

"Saying your car's out there," Tina interpreted unnecessarily, for the pantomime had been plain enough, "so you should be home."

A few more words and the grey-haired man climbed into the black saloon, reversed in the confined space with the practiced ease of one who has performed the same or similar manoeuvres many times before, and drove away through the arch. The younger man, left alone, rubbed his lumpy chin thoughtfully and then moved towards the staircase. A few seconds later came a tattoo on the door, followed by a deep voice calling: "Howell, you in there? Open up if you are!" Then came a silence. After a while he reappeared in the courtyard, making his way slowly back, presumably to his own flat.

"And that's that," Tina remarked. "Give him a few minutes and I'll be off on my shopping spree. I should be able to slip out without him or anyone else seeing me. In the meantime I'll use your bathroom. To powder my nose, as nice girls say."

An operation that took all of ten minutes. But then it appeared she had been carrying the essentials of comb, lipstick and compact in one of the pockets of her black slacks.

"All clear?" She went into the bedroom to check at the window. "All clear. I won't be long, Howie-boy. Don't leave the country or go back to school or anything while I'm gone, will you?" And then, from the hall, with a change of voice: "Come here, Howie."

He hurried after her. She pointed down to the slip of folded paper that had been pushed under the door. "It'll be for you. No doubt left by curly-nob."

Howell, it read, *Doc Wharton wants you should see him as soon as possible. Urgent, he says.* And it was signed: *Pete*.

"I told you he wasn't a lawyer," Tina said, as if he had argued with her about it. "Sounds like you've been under the doctor. You look well enough to me. Right—" She opened the door. "Here we go."

Closing the door behind her, Howell returned to the bedroom, from where he could keep an eye on the courtyard. He turned from watching Tina's slim shape hurry, almost run, through the arch, to gaze reflectively at the bottom drawer of the dressing table. It was time, he felt, to do some thinking about all that money. On the telly, brief cases packed with used notes were almost always to do with one of two things, either blackmail or kidnap. But the amounts then were always in nice round figures, five thousand, say, or ten. That odd three hundred put this money here into a different category. Unless it had originally been a round figure, and a start had been made on spending it. Sixteen, then, but even that sounded wrong. Villains on the telly always seemed to work in units of five.

So what, then? Not honest savings, not hidden away in a locked drawer instead of earning interest in a bank. Which left only the proceeds of a robbery. But who had robbed whom or what? The Howell of now might be a changed person from the Howie of '69, but one thing was for sure, and that was that he would never have anything to do with any kind of robbery. Neither would Mick Debroy. Which meant a third party had to be involved. But that wasn't the answer either. Neither he nor Mick were prigs or anything like that, but he was damn' well sure neither of them would knowingly allow stolen money to be dumped in the flat. Unless—and this was a disturbing notion—Mick had changed drastically over the last five years. Suppose he had. All right. So why, if all that money belonged to Mick, had he still gone on living here in this shabby little joint? And why had he now presumably gone away leaving the money behind?

Engrossed in his thoughts Howell didn't know that Tina had returned. Her knock startled him. He didn't have to ask who it was. "Knock three times and ask for Susie," her voice, rather breathless, came from outside. Breathless because she had been hurrying. "I ran here from the arch so's nobody would see me." Her arms were clasped about a huge plastic bag covered with a psychodelic pattern of impossible flowers and birds, glaring colours that shrieked to heaven. "Not been long, have I? There's a nice small self-service just round the corner."

She piled cartons, bags, jars and cans on the kitchen table. "For dinner, curried chicken with rice; how does that hit you? Fruit salad and cream for afters." Enough stuff, it seemed to Howell, to feed a fair-sized family for a week.

"And a special offer here on soap powder. Your pal Howell can do some of his own laundry for a change. Oh, and I got this; I don't suppose you thought about getting one of these." A small electric torch. "For your breaking and entering, yes? And here's your change. I had to break into both notes."

73

She began stacking the things away in the cupboard. "There's a telephone kiosk round the corner, too. You don't have a phone in here, do you?"

He didn't know offhand. But if there had been a telephone in the place he would surely have noticed it.

"I didn't want to call anyone," Tina explained. "Just use the directory. An idea I got." She looked back over her shoulder to watch his reaction. "Find out where Dr. Wharton has his surgery. Two of 'em in the book, one out Hampstead way, the other here in S.E. fifteen." She paused, eyeing him with some wariness. "I thought perhaps it might have been in Gladwyn Place."

He smiled to let her know he was in no way ruffled.

"I told you that room wasn't a doctor's surgery," he pointed out mildly.

"But judging by that note pushed under the door you have been under the doctor." Having stowed all the food away she closed the cupboard and stepped back. "That man who was with the doctor, the one who wrote the note, he must be a friend of yours by the way he signed himself 'Pete.' I think I liked the look of him. Nice and big-brotherish in a lumpy sort of way. Lives about three doors down so far as I could tell." She looked at her watch. "Half past three. Fancy a cup of tea, Howie?"

She brought it, and a packet of biscuits, to where he sat on the worn rust-coloured settee in the lounge. "Not only no phone," she observed, "no telly nor radio neither. Talk about being cut off. I wonder what you and your friend Mick used to do those nights you stayed home?" She grinned cheerfully at him over the rim of her cup. "I mean, you did once used to be at school together."

He didn't get her meaning at first. When he did he flushed, becoming too embarrassed even to be angry. She viewed his discomfort with some surprise. "We are touchy, aren't we? I was only trying to be funny, for Susan's sake. Although there's so much homo and lessie stuff knocking about these days it's hardly worth joking about any more." She put her head on one

74

side. "You are really still only a schoolboy inside, aren't you, Howie?"

He wasn't offended at what was after all no more than the truth.

"I'll have to try and catch up on those five years," he said wryly. "With your help I stand a fair chance of doing it."

Tina finished her tea, dusted crumbs from the pleasantly curved front of her white jumper and leaned back, yawning and stretching. "I could use a nap. Half past eight, you said we move off, didn't you? That means I'll have to start putting dinner together at about seven. I hope you're not expecting anything too fancy—"

Curried chicken, even out of a packet, was a very happy change after the unimaginative school meals of lumpy gravy, soggy potatoes, overdone meat and underdone greens. There was even a bottle of wine. With no corkscrew to be found in the place, they had to dig the cork out in pieces with the opened prongs of a fork.

Impatient to be on the move, too early even though he knew it to be, Howell would have left the dirty dishes piled in the sink. Tina insisted they leave the place as they had found it . . . "If possible, a little cleaner, and that shouldn't be too difficult. You wouldn't want Howell to come back to find the place looking like a pigsty, would you?"

They left at about quarter past eight. With no road map to help him, Howell intended feeling his way slowly through the surrounding maze of side streets, aiming in the general direction of Surbiton. Once he hit the A240 there, everything would be plain sailing.

Tina checked from one of the bedroom windows. "Nobody about. I think they must all be dead, I've never come across such a quiet joint." But as they reached the bottom of the echoing iron steps, a woman with a basket in one hand and a leash-straining white poodle attached to the other, came bustling through the arch. Clearly a resident, a neighbour, and Howell, knowing that something would be expected of him, nodded and smiled and ostentatiously quickened his pace, hoping that by giving the impression of being in a hurry he would discourage any idea the woman might have of stopping to chat.

But that was very obviously the last thing she had in mind. She answered his smile and nod with a bare inclination of her head, looked quickly away and quickened her own pace, dragging the dog closer to her side.

As they passed through the arch Tina looked back over her shoulder, reporting: "Next door to you, Howie." And puzzled: "You'd have thought she'd have been friendlier than that, wouldn't you?" And something else. "That's a bit like what they were at the party. You know, I told you they were sort of politely distant towards you, like they didn't seem all that keen on being pally.

"And as for that woman—" They had reached the car; Tina turned to look back again. "If I'm any judge of faces, I'd say she seemed almost—*frightened*—of you."

Howell turned from opening the car door to exclaim harshly: "That's stupid!" But there could be no denying that by the look on the woman's face she had felt far from happy at even such a brief, passing contact.

He pointed the bonnet to where he judged the south to be. At a gargage where he stopped for petrol he asked the way, finding he had been going in the wrong direction. Consequently it was over an hour before they reached Surbiton and the familiar A240. Forty minutes later, dusk settling over the fields and trees of what was now open country, and they were on the outskirts of Epsom. Another fifteen minutes, half past ten now, dark, and they had arrived at Gretton.

7

HOWELL, DRIVING SLOWLY, POINTED OUT such land-marks as could be identified at that time of night.

"That's our church." On the left, some distance back from the road, growing from a dark mystery of trees, a squat square tower outlined against the stars. "I was christened there."

Tina had had very little to say for herself on the journey down. He had been grateful for her silence, not yet at home with the car, not experienced enough in any case to be able to drive automatically with his mind on other things.

"You've always lived here, then?" she wondered, not sounding to be all that interested.

"Apart from when I'm away at school." He pointed to the other side of the road. "Over there. You can just about make out the roofs of the plant over the hedge. Those two long buildings, see?"

Tina was surprised. "Is that all? Just those two buildings? Is that all Trowman Chemicals is? It's not very big, is it?"

He laughed at her, the first time he had laughed in a long time. "This is just the Fine Drugs Plant here in Gretton. Our real factories are just outside Birmingham. We only make some of the more expensive drugs here. They're labs, really. They do research here. Here's the works entrance now." Not very large double gates on the right, heavily shaded by trees. "The office has its own entrance about quarter of a mile further on, but we turn off before then."

They passed between neat rows of semi-detached houses, black cut-out bushes in tiny front gardens, cosy lights glowing through net curtains.

"This is where the workmen live and some of the office staff." Howell watched the dolls' houses slide by. "We helped pay to have them built."

He slowed to a crawl to take an almost concealed turning on the left. There had been a few lights along the road they had just left, here there were none at all. The narrow road, little more than a lane, snaked between high hedgerows, that on the left ending abruptly at a pair of white-painted wooden gates.

"Home, sweet home," he said, but drove on past, explaining: "There's another gate further on, much closer to the house."

Wrought-iron gates this time, with behind them, a gravel drive leading away to the shadowy shape of quite a large house. He pulled up a few yards away. "Here we are, then."

The girl turned to look back over her shoulder, found nothing to see—the house having become hidden again by the tall hedge —and turned back to the front again, looking to be far from feeling at ease. So worried, in fact, that Howell, about to open his door, paused, leaning forward the better to make out her features, not all that clear in the dim interior light, asking her if anything was the matter.

"All this—" She broke off, paused, started again. "I've got a feeling this isn't a very clever thing to do, Howie."

Puzzled by her sudden concern, he tried to reassure her. "Sneak into the place, you mean? I don't much care for it myself, but it's the best way. Just in case. And even if I am spotted, I should be able to talk my way out of it without things getting beyond me. If Dad's still here, and working, I'll see his light and come back here and try again later. I'm not doing anything wrong, you know. It is my own home. There's no need to worry."

"It's not that." She stared ahead through the windscreen. "There's something—*wrong* about all this. Something very wrong. Frightening. I don't mean because of the way that woman looked at you or because of all that money in your flat or anything like that. It's something I thought of coming down. Something you couldn't have thought of else you'd have said. That flat of yours, Howie; I'm sure someone must have gone through it, taking away anything that might give you any clue as to the name of the man you're sharing with. It was only by luck they overlooked that old envelope pinned in the cupboard. Well, don't you see, for them to have done all that means they must have known what had happened to you, see? They must have known you no longer knew who you were sharing with. Otherwise there'd have been no point in removing all trace of him, see?"

Howell did see, and spent a few moments getting it sorted out in his mind. It made sense, and yet at the same time it was impossible. Because—

"Nobody apart from you knows what has happened to me. You're the only one I've spoken to. There's no way in which they could have found out." And there was something else, something even more impossible. "Judging by the dust in the flat, nobody could have been there for some time. Which means they must have searched the place before I came here to this time, while I was still back at school."

"It doesn't so much matter when," Tina said. "They *knew*—that's what's important. And there's only one way in which they could know. They must have been the people who've done this to you—done something to you to make you believe you've come from the past. I don't know how. You read about such things; more often than not you don't believe any of it. Maybe they got hold of you, drugged you or something, took you to that room, put the notion in your head you were back at school and five years younger, then left you to wake up, maybe with a message in your mind telling you to leave the room the moment you did come round. It could have been like that, I suppose. I can't possibly imagine why they've done it. Maybe they want you to lead them somewhere or to something. Something only you know about." She warmed to the notion. "Some sort of secret. Something very important for them to have gone to all this trouble. Perhaps something only you know about on account of you being Trowman's son." She gestured helplessly. "I don't know. But I do know that something was done to you between that party last night and you waking up in that room. What d'you think, Howie?"

He smiled down at her. "That you've been watching too much blood-and-thunder telly."

She bridled at his tone, becoming indignant. "So it's far out. So it's not nearly as far out as your story about travelling through time. At least mine is possible."

"I suppose it is," he conceded, refusing to be sidetracked into an old argument. "All the same, I think you're wrong about the flat having been deliberately stripped of everything that might tell me who's living there with me. Why should anyone want to stop me finding out it's just an old school friend? And why go to all that trouble anyway when all I have to do is ask one of the neighbours?"

"I hadn't thought of that. Perhaps they put a message in your mind telling you not to. Well, you were against me asking them, weren't you?" She half turned in her seat to gaze back in the direction of the invisible house. "Going in there might be just what they want you to do, Howie."

"I'm leading them, whoever they might be, to some sort of trade secret." He considered that possibility. "Yes, that could be on the books if I was working for my father, even more so if I'd taken over from him. There are secrets to do with new preparations that rival concerns, Solmex in particular, would pay a lot of money to find out about before they're put on the market. But nothing like that is ever kept in the house. It's all in the safes across at the labs, and I've no intention of going there. Too big a risk, apart from anything else. Especially if, as you say, I'm working for Solmex and, if appearances are anything to go by, nobody of any great importance."

"At least nobody's followed us here. Once I'd figured out what might be going on I kept my eye on the road behind."

He opened the door.

"Be careful," she warned anxiously as he stepped out into

the lane. "How will you get in—climb on a roof and through an upstairs window?"

"There's three french windows in the lounge. On the far one, the beading's loose inside. If you slide something thin through the crack you can push the beading away and lift the catch."

She thrust her head through the open window, reluctant, it seemed, to let him go; thinking of excuses to keep him there. "Have you got the torch?"

He took it out of his pocket ready. "But I will need something to open the door with. I should have thought to bring a table knife. Do you happen to have a longish nail file?"

She hadn't; neither was there anything in the car that would serve the purpose. Howell wasn't concerned. "There's bound to be something in the garage. I'll go there first; the doors are never locked."

He pushed open one side of the iron gates. It felt strange to be creeping into his own home like this, sneaking up the drive like a thief, afraid of being spotted. Because he knew of this special way of getting into the house unobserved didn't mean he had ever made use of it before at night. He had used the french window before, but only during the daytime and for no other reason than, still very much a schoolboy, it had been great fun to be able to get into the house like a burglar, without anyone else knowing.

The drive curved and the whole front of the house was in view, exactly the same as he remembered it, unchanged from the last time he had been here, a couple of months ago in the Easter break. No—five years and two months ago.

All the windows were in darkness. Either they were out, in one of the rooms overlooking the lawn at the back, or else in bed. He flashed the torch on his watch. Quarter to eleven. Neither Mother nor Dad had ever been in the habit of keeping late hours when they were at home. The odds were they were both in bed.

He moved towards the squat bulk of the garage on the right, not part of the main building but separated from it by a path that led to the gardens at the rear. He tested the doors, found them unlocked as he had expected, and opened one of them just wide enough for him to skip into the petrol- and oil-smelling interior.

The lay-out of the place had been the same for as long as he could remember. Mother's little Austin, used for visiting and general running about, was always kept on the right, Father's big show-off Rolls on the left. Now, the Austin space was empty—perhaps Mother was away—and Dad had changed his Rolls for—Howell swung the beam of his torch on the bonnet —an Aston Martin. An expensive-looking job in pale blue with a snazzy interior. But he wasn't here to inspect cars. He went to the far end of the building, to the long bench that occupied the full length of the wall. There was nothing among the tools and odds and ends scattered on the bench that would serve his purpose. Stooping, he dragged out one of the heavy metal tool chests from underneath and raised the lid. He found what he was looking for under another of his school scarves—another bought one, not knitted—and a bundle of greasy rags. From a selection of various tools he chose a screwdriver with a thin shaft.

Closing the garage door behind him he made his way silently along the front of the house to the far one of the three french windows. It was only when he came to use the torch to show him where to insert the screwdriver that the thought occurred to him that it was possible that during the past five years the faulty beading might have been spotted and repaired.

But it hadn't. The screwdriver slid in easily, slid upwards easily, clicked gently against the latch and raised it effortlessly. Slipping the tool into his pocket Howell opened the window and stepped into the room.

The door of the room that had been converted into an office was on the left-hand wall. Another quick flash of the torch in that direction showed him that a chair was in his way, a winged chair that he couldn't recall having seen before, and so must be a new acquisition. He patted its high curved back on his way to the door. Another door that was never locked, for, apart from a policy of always trusting the servants, and letting them know they were trusted, nothing of value, nothing worth stealing was ever kept inside.

It was still unlocked. A slow sweep of the torch showed him that here there had been quite a few changes. Dad's big bureau that had always stood across the opposite corner was no longer there. Instead, a large desk sat squarely in the centre of the room. A metal filing cabinet was new, as were also the shelves filled with files. Still, what was it the French said? The more things change, the more they stay the same. Or something like that.

His torch had covered the room from where he stood in the doorway. It had left undiscovered anything that might be on either side of that doorway. His interest centred on the desk, he stepped into the room. His foot caught against some kind of obstruction. From the corner of his eye he caught the flicker of movement of something falling, but, swinging sharply round, was too late to stop whatever it was from hitting the floor. The thud of something heavy striking the carpet, muted and dull as it was, seemed to him to echo through the whole place. He froze where he stood, listening, his pulse racing and his heart thumping as if he were indeed an intruder in a strange house, a burglar who, if caught, would be held while the police were sent for.

The house remained silent. The noise didn't seem to have been heard by any of the occupants. He swung the torch on the cause—a mahogany pedestal, an ugly affair, still upright, and on the floor the bust it had supported—Shakespeare, by the look of it, the very last thing he would have expected the old man to have in his office. Setting the torch on the floor he replaced the bust, picked up the torch again and went across to the desk.

The top was clear apart from a brown folder. He opened it, holding the torch low to help him make out the small print. Details of some kind of staff re-organisation. Having to hold the torch meant having to work clumsily one-handed. He looked up from reading, wondering if he dare risk switching on the room lights.

While he hesitated, the decision was taken from him. Light came flooding through the doorway of the lounge from the lights that had been switched on in there. Not by any of the servants; they slept at the rear of the house, they'd never have heard the noise that damn' bust made. Either Mother or Dad. He hoped it was Mother.

And: "Tompkin?" a woman's voice called. A voice he knew but for a moment couldn't place. "Is that you, puss?"

He still couldn't place it when she came to stand in the doorway, but then the light was behind her, her features in shadow. But it wasn't Mother—she was slender. This woman was short and dumpy. Then, still not seeing him standing there behind the desk—he had automatically switched off the torch at the first sound of her voice—she moved to one side. He saw her face in the same moment she saw him.

"Aunt Meg!" he exclaimed, of the two the least surprised; she and Uncle Wilf often stayed at Ferncroft.

She was startled, naturally enough. "Howell?" As if she couldn't believe her eyes. Her voice rose in disbelief. "It is you, Howell?" She came a step nearer so that now she could see him clearly. "Howell!" she said again, and this time there seemed something more than startlement in her tone. And it seemed to him too that the new expression that had come to her eyes was the same as that which had been in the eyes of the woman with the poodle back in the courtyard. The woman Tina had said had shown fear of him.

Impossible then, even more impossible now. Aunt Meg, afraid of him. Grey-haired—in rollers, now, and covered with a chiffon scarf—round pink face and china-blue eyes, fluttery and helpless—wearing a pink nightdress of some woolly material as old-fashioned as the hills, enveloping her from neck to toe.

"What are you doing here?" she asked, and he had never heard her use such a sharp tone before. And then, not giving him any chance to reply, looking apprehensively up at the ceiling: "I only hope Wilfred didn't hear you." "Wilfred," not "Uncle Wilf," and that didn't make sense. Unless the Howell of now had become too grown-up to have an aunt and uncle who weren't really relatives.

She lowered her gaze from the ceiling. "I thought I heard him . . . You shouldn't have come here, Howell. You ought to have known better." Her voice little more than an urgent whisper. "I don't know what you could have been thinking of. If he—"

"Margaret?" Uncle Wilf's voice, coming from somewhere upstairs, or perhaps from somewhere on the staircase. "Margaret? What's going on down there?"

"Nothing!" she called back, and took hold of Howell's arm, urging him towards the door. "Quickly, in case he comes down. He mustn't find you here." There could be no denying the urgency she was feeling. If she hadn't been afraid before, she certainly was now. Afraid, for God's sake, of what dithering, ineffectual old Uncle Wilf would say or do if he came down to find him here? It didn't make sense, none of it, their being here, no sign of Mother or Dad.

"Where's—" he started.

But she silenced him with her hand over his mouth, whispering urgently: "How did you get in here?"

He showed her, pointing to the window, still open.

She urged him towards it. "Quickly. I think he's coming down." She looked back over her shoulder. "I don't know what he'll do if he finds you here."

Dazed, he allowed himself to be hustled through the window —hustled by Aunt Meg, who usually was so afraid of causing offence she would never so much as shoo a bird away—hustled out of the house and into the night as if he were a stranger and this not his own home. Even before he could stop and turn, the lights went out in the room—she must have run over to the switch to have done it so quickly. He caught the sound of Uncle Wilf's voice, but not what he was saying, as he turned to make his way down the drive to where Tina waited in the car, pleased and surprised to see him—pleased that he had returned safely, surprised because: "I thought you would have been much longer. Did you find what you wanted?"

He didn't reply until he had slid into his seat, turned the car round, a difficult manoeuvre for him in the narrow lane with much bumping over grassy verges, and was driving back the way they had come. Then he told her what had happened, even now he had had time to think about, still unable to make any sense of it, unable to imagine what could possibly have come over Aunt Meg to change her so much.

"She was the one who was always so fond of me, all over me, you know? Even more than Mother. I used to hate her coming to see me at school because of the fuss she always made. And in there now she just couldn't get rid of me fast enough." He didn't mention anything about the fear she had shown.

"And nothing about your own people?" Tina wondered.

He shook his head. "Not a word. I don't think they could have been home. In fact I'm sure they couldn't. Maybe Aunt Meg and Uncle Wilf are staying there while they're away somewhere." He didn't sound to be at all happy with that explanation. "All the same—"

Tina broke into what he had been about to say. "Pull up here, Howie." And when he had automatically obeyed: "What's the time?" The dashboard clock wasn't going. She held her wrist to the light. "Nearly eleven. Is that when pubs close out here in the wilds?"

Still occupied with other things, he didn't know what she was on about. "You mean you want a drink?"

"I don't want a drink." She opened her door. "Just back there we passed the local Pig and Whistle. Still lit up." And then her reason for having told him to stop: "If ever you want to know what's going on in a place, always go to the local boozer. Didn't you know that? Regular mines of information, they are."

She climbed out of the car. "I'll watch my step," she promised as she reached in the back for her coat. Draping it over her shoulders she walked back down in the road in the direction of a cluster of small buildings—some of the original cottages of the village, Howell recalled—one of them the thatched, pretty-pretty inn with a name he couldn't for the moment remember.

Welcoming a time in which to think, he closed his eyes and leaned back. There was no trouble in painting Aunt Meg's face on the dark screen of his closed lids. And so had it been fear, that look in her eyes? Hard to say with any certainty now. But Aunt Meg afraid of him? The very idea was ludicrous.

86

But there was something now that he had time to think. Her surprise at seeing him there in the office had been in two parts, as it were. There had been the first shock at finding anyone at all, then a few moments of getting over it, and then a second dose of surprise, as if he were the very last person she had expected to see, as if his own home was the very last place he ought to be. Which might mean he no longer lived there, that he had left home, that that poky little flat in Pickham was his home now. And that was another stupid notion. He could think of nothing, however bad, that would ever make him—or the Howell of now, come to that—kick over the traces and leave home completely. That idea was out of the question.

Tina returned much sooner than he had expected. The tapping of her high heels brought him out of a drifting of ideas that was leading nowhere. He opened the door for her.

"Called the Barn Owl," she informed him brightly as she settled in her seat. "Nice little place by the look."

And her look, her tone and the way she avoided his eyes, told him she had something she would rather not tell him.

"Dad," he said, barely making a question of it.

"I'm sorry," she told the windscreen. "Just a couple of months ago, the man said. I'm sorry, Howie."

"I think I knew all the time. A sort of feeling . . ." He rested his hands on the wheel as if by so doing the contact with the cold plastic would help steady his voice. He took a deep breath. "Only two months ago?"

She nodded. "Sinclair. That's the name of the people who have the house now."

"Aunt Meg and Uncle Wilf. You mean, they live there now?"

"They bought it after your father died. He thinks your mother's in Switzerland. He's not sure. Abroad somewhere, anyway."

She turned to look at him, her eyes dark with sympathy, gently putting her hand on his where it rested on the rim of the wheel. "And that's all, Howie. I'm afraid that's all I was able to find out. I got the door slammed in my face after that." She seemed to be spinning the thing out to give him time in which to recover. "You ever had that happen to you? It's not much fun. You sort of get the feeling nobody loves you. I only just stepped back in time, otherwise my nose would have suffered. And all I did was ask the man if he knew what had become of Mr. Trowman's son."

Tina paused reflectively. "The funny thing is, by the way he'd been eyeing me all the time—wary, you know?—I got the feeling that that was what he'd been waiting for, me to start asking about you. He went all nasty, said if I was a reporter he knew how to deal with that breed, and then he banged the door right in my face. A reporter . . ." She paused again. "That means newspapers, some sort of story. Now what do you suppose—"

But Howell wasn't listening. Opening his door he stepped out of the car to walk slowly along the road away from the village. He stopped at a gap in the ragged hedge, going to rest his arms along the top of the wooden gate that spanned it. The sky was still clear and high. A half-moon had come to join the stars and lay a silver gloss on the roofs over on the left. The roofs of the labs, the first buildings Dad bought, the start of it all.

He was dead. The Old Man was dead. Two months ago. May, that would have been. The Merry Month of May.

Something, some animal or other, rustled urgently in the hedge. There was a rich smell of grass. Cut grass that had been drying in the sun. Harvest. The fields behind the house, too small for a combine to be worth hiring, so cut by a rattling machine pulled by a chugging tractor, and then stacked by hand. The Old Man there working, enjoying every minute, faded khaki shorts and shirt open to the waist, taking a turn at driving the tractor, swinging a pitchfork, face the scarlet of the sunset. Like a schoolboy.

And now the lonely night.

All in the Merrie Month of May. Oh, Dad—

The more things change, the more they remain the same. That was a laugh.

After a time, how long he didn't know, Howell walked slowly back to where Tina waited patiently in the car. Asking anxiously: "All right, Howie?" as he lowered himself to his seat.

He smiled and nodded. "All right."

"It's not fair."

"What isn't? Dad being dead? It was always on the cards; I told you that."

"No, not so much that. You having to go through it all twice, you know? It must have been just as bad for you the first time you were told. It's not right you should have to suffer it all again."

"I know when he died." He stared through the windscreen at the ragged outline of the hedge against the sky. "So do I get sent back to my own time knowing when it was, and have to live through the five years before it happens, knowing exactly when it will happen, and having to keep it to myself? I don't think I could do that. I only hope to God that whoever brought me here will do something about wiping my memory clean before sending me back."

He shrugged his blue serge-covered shoulders. "Still, that's neither here nor there. What's to be, will be. So he died in May, Mother left the country, and Uncle Wilf and Aunt Meg bought the house and are living there now. You didn't happen to find out who took over from Dad as head of the firm?"

She shook her head. "I've told you everything. Except it was your Dad's heart, but I suppose you'd already guessed that. Oh—and except that judging by the way that man at the pub acted, there must have been some sort of story to do with you that found its way into the papers. Big news, by the sound of it. I mean, there was the way, the moment I brought your name into it, he said he knew how to handle reporters. Like he'd had a hell of a lot to do with them."

"Something about me in the papers . . ." Howell sought inspiration from the roof light. "When the old man died, instead of me going into the firm, for some reason or other I went to work for Solmex. Or if I was already working for the old man, I chucked it in when he died." He turned to look at her. "Either way, it would have made news."

She studied his face. "But you don't think that was it?"

"I can't see it being important enough to bring reporters buzzing about the place."

Tina hunched her shoulders, clasping her hands in her lap as if suddenly cold. "So there's one mystery here, and another back at your flat—that money, and your friend Mick, who seems to be missing without trace. Two different things, d'you think, Howie? Or all part of the same one?"

"That's what I've got to try to find out." A breeze moved the top of the hedge and the shape made by one of the gently waving silhouetted branches became that of a witch riding a broomstick. "So far it's been all deadends. I don't know where to try next. Yet with all the people I used to know, surely there's someone else I can go to."

There was. Thinking about Mick Debroy brought another face to mind. A thin ugly face between rough towel-scarf and hair still wet and spiked from the showers.

"Andy," Howell said.

"And who's he when he's at home?" Tina wanted to know.

"Andrew Brett. He was with Mick and me at school. We were all prefects. I was talking to both of them this morning, just before all this happened. Mick told me he'd got himself a job with Solmex, and Andy came to remind me to speak to Dad about finding him a spot with our firm. He'd asked me several times before. I said I'd do what I could."

"So he may be working for your firm now?"

"If Dad was in a good mood. Usually he didn't go in for that sort of thing—jobs for the boys. He liked to leave the question of staff to his personnel people. But I'd never asked him a favour like that before, so I stood a reasonable chance of him saying yes. Chemistry wasn't one of Andy's strong points, so he won't have gone into either the labs here or the factory at Birmingham. Advertising or administration, he said. And if he's in either of those, his place will be here at the Hall. And he'll owe me a good turn. Not that I'll have to wave that in his face. So now I have to find out what my persuasive powers were like five years back."

Tina held her watch to the light again. "At this time of night?"

"There's always someone at the Hall, day and night. I doubt whether any of the staff will be working this late, but there'll be a night porter on duty, always is." He reached for the starter. "He'll know the names of everyone working there." The engine came to life. He paused with his hand over the gear lever.

"Will he know you?" Tina asked, watching his face.

"Used to be a man called Richardson. Ex-army type. Been there for years, more than likely he's still there." Howell nodded shortly. "If it is him, he'll know me the moment he claps eyes on me."

"And maybe react the same way your aunt did," she supplied.

"That's what I was thinking," he agreed wryly. "It looks like I seem to have done a real good job of upsetting all and sundry. I only hope to God I haven't trodden on Andy's toes as well."

"Muggins again, then?"

He knew what she meant. "I am sorry you have to keep on doing my dirty work for me, Tina." He sounded as if he really meant it and was not merely being polite.

"It can't be any worse than the last door-slammed-in-the-face effort. At least I can't blame you for that—I volunteered. So I'm volunteering again. Here—" She held out her hand.

He reached across to take hold of it with his right hand, smiling sideways, asking: "You're not saying good-bye, just to be on the safe side?"

"Nothing so drastic. No." She became formal. "How do you do. My name is Christine Martin. I'm very pleased to meet you."

"And what was that in aid of?"

She let go his hand. "I was just introducing myself to the new Howell Trowman. The grown-up one. He grew up a little while back. Before that he was only a schoolboy, doing his best to act like a man. And not making too bad a job of it either."

He shook his head at her. "You're a funny girl," he told her, and made a very neat job of reversing the car in only two manoeuvres. "What will you say to the porter?"

"I'm getting good at this. Oh—smile sweetly at him—I'm good at that, too—apologise for disturbing him so late—was just driving through when I remembered a friend of a friend by the name of Andy something-or-other—"

"Brett."

"Thanks. Andy Brett worked here and thought it would be nice to look him up. And what d'you mean, me a funny girl?"

"In the very nicest sort of way," he assured her.

They passed the left-hand turn that led to Howell's one-time home. Now there were more semi-detached houses on either side. When they came to an end, neatly trimmed hedges appeared. Howell pulled in to the side, his near-side wheels bumping over the grass verge, the car canted at an angle. Switching off the engine he pointed to where, a few yards ahead, light spilled out onto the road.

"That's the Hall entrance. The porter's lodge is on the left. You'll see a bell-push on the gate."

"Ta." She climbed out. "Just call me Mata Hari. Be seeing you."

He watched her down the road, slender under the lights, scarlet coat swinging from narrow shoulders. Her hips were just the right shape to fit into slacks, neither too plump nor too flat and possessed of a very enticing sway.

Shifting in his seat brought something to press painfully into his side. He had forgotten about the screwdriver he had slipped into his jacket pocket after using it to open the french windows. Not Dad's screwdriver, as he had first thought, but Uncle Wilf's.

Dad . . . At school, afraid it might be considered childish if he were to call him that when talking about him to the other boys, he had tried to copy the other seniors by calling him "The Old Man." But it had never caught on. He found himself using both names in both conversation and thoughts.

It wouldn't do any good thinking about him now. But it seemed wrong to deliberately try to forget him, even though, as Tina had said, he had gone through all this before, must have done. Once before, someone else had had to break the news to him, just like Tina had a while back. Perhaps Mother, that other time. A strange notion. But just because he had mourned once already didn't mean he could turn it off now like—like turning off a light. The pain would dull after a while, just as it must have done once already, or started to, anyway. If Dad had only been gone a couple of months, then the Howell of now must still be feeling it.

Tossing the screwdriver into the glove compartment, he climbed stiffly out of the car to stand looking along the road towards the pale flood of light that marked the entrance to the Hall, wondering, hoping one train of thought would submerge another, how Tina was making out.

He heard the sound of her returning footsteps before he saw the girl herself. But then she had been walking in the shadow of the hedge, only moving out to the centre of the road when she saw he was out of the car and standing by it.

"Mission accomplished." She treated him to an exaggerated version of an American-style throw-away salute. "But not without some danger. Funny little man with greasy hair, a flashy bow tie and a roving eye. The sort it's best to keep your bottom turned away from—well, mine, anyway—in case he has any Italian ideas."

Howell smiled at her description. "That's Richardson, right enough. The local dirty old man. He also rings the bells at that church I showed you. Used to, anyway."

"My, my. Village life in the raw. Well, he knew all about your friend without having to look him up or anything. Mr. Brett works in something called Urgent Delivery, Serums and Vaccines, and lodges along the road here with people called Humphrey at—what was the number—twenty-three." She ended with another salute. "How's that, sir?"

"Fine." Howell turned to look along the road. "It'll be one of the houses just past the Epsom road opening. Only a few yards, we can walk it."

"He'll probably have turned in. It's almost half past eleven. This is the country, not the town."

"If he has gone to bed, he won't mind turning out again for me."

"You hope," Tina said with a certain significance.

"Yes," Howell agreed soberly. "I hope."

Number twenty-three was the end house of the row, an

ordinary semi-detached, no different from any of its companions, even with the same pocket-handkerchief front lawn, grey in the red glow that filtered through the drawn curtains of the downstairs bow window.

"At least they're still up," Tina observed as he opened the gate for her to precede him up the narrow flagged drive. "And they've not got their noses glued to the telly. Unless they're watching with the lights on."

They weren't. It appeared the occupants of the front room were playing cards. The man who opened the door to Howell's knock had brought his hand with him, fanned in front of his unbuttoned waistcoat. By his voice and expression he was anything but pleased at having to interrupt his game.

"Mr. Brett?" He nodded curtly at Howell's opening enquiry. "Ay, 'e's our lodger. But 'e ain't down, 'e went up a bit ago. Gettin' on."

Apologetically, Howell said he knew it was late. But Mr. Brett was a very old friend of his. "We were just passing through"—remembering the excuse Tina had used to preface her enquiries at the Hall. "We might not have a chance to see him again."

"Ay." Considering the point, Mr. Humphrey scratched his chin with his playing-card fan, tuning his bald head to look up the narrow staircase behind him. "Likely 'e ain't in kip yet." And turning back: "Wot name shall I say?"

Howell's hesitation was barely noticeable. "Just tell him it's an old school friend."

Mr. Humphrey didn't invite them in, left them standing in the tiny vestibule while he lumbered up the stairs. There was a rap on a door, a murmur of voices, then he came back down again to report: "Down in a minnit." And then, still leaving them standing there outside, went back to his interrupted game.

And after a while, there was Andy, unchanged, just as he had always been, not looking to be any older even, hair tousled, still as ugly as ever, even managing to give the impression of loping rather than walking as he came slowly down the stairs, not looking where he was going, busy with the ties of his blue dressing-gown, not looking up until he had reached the hall and was there in front of them.

A moment of puzzlement then, for the girl was the first person his gaze rested on. Then it shifted, and he was looking at Howell, and his expression was changing. From mild perplexity to astonishment; and from that, all in the same moment, to something very different—the expression of someone looking at something he would rather not see, that he had no time for, that he loathed and detested. No fear in his face—instead, hatred and bitterness.

And a voice to match, so harsh and grating when he spoke that it wasn't Andy's voice at all.

"What the hell are you doing here, Trowman?"

Not "Howie"; not even "Howell." "Trowman."

"I'm sorry—" Howell faltered, shaken by that expression and that tone. And that was as far as he was allowed to get.

"You've got one hell of a bloody nerve coming here." Andy's voice rose, trembling, actually shaking with what was certainly suppressed anger. "I don't know what you're after, and I don't bloody well care. I don't want to hear anything you have to say. Get the hell out of here before I lose my temper and do something I might be sorry for."

His gaze moved momentarily to Tina's startled face. His voice softened a fraction. "Whoever you are, I'm sorry," he said, and closed the door in front of them.

"And that," Tina said in a small unsteady voice, "is what it feels like to have a door slammed in your face."

8

THEY WALKED BACK TO THE CAR in silence. And reaching it, Howell opening the door for her, there was no discussion as to what their next move should be, both of them seeming to take it for granted that they wouldn't try to find beds for the night in Gretton but, late as the hour was—getting on for midnight, now—they would drive back to London.

They passed nothing at all along the five-mile stretch of road that linked Gretton with the A240. And there wasn't all that much traffic once they reached that road, with the bonnet now pointing north towards Surbiton. Howell, still not wholly able to drive automatically, tucked himself in behind a fairly fast-moving van with corrugated aluminium sides. Tina finally broke the silence to read aloud from the gaudy advertisement adorning the van's high rear.

"'Buckley's Betta Bickies.' Yuk. Enough to put anyone off. But it must pay; you see their biscuits everywhere."

"They sell them in our school tuck shop," Howell said.

"Did you really have a tuck shop? I didn't think there were such things, not really, only in stories about schools."

"We have one."

She was silent for a second or two. Then: "You did say that man, Andy Brett, was a friend of yours at school?"

"He was," Howell said drily. "Not what you might call close, but still, a friend. You wouldn't have thought so a while back, would you?"

"By the way he acted, you must have done something more than just step on his toes."

"I've never seen Andy in such a state before." Howell's tone was as bleak as his face. "I've never even seen him get ruffled, let alone lose his temper. But back there—" He shook his head in a kind of wonderment, momentarily lost for words. "Like he hated my very guts. Like if you hadn't been there he might even have had a go at tossing me out on my ear. Andy . . . I just can't believe it. I wish to God I knew what it was all about."

"Whatever it is," Tina reasoned, "it must have been really foul. And big enough to affect quite a lot of people and even get into the papers. That's if it's all the same thing, and I suppose it must be."

"Two of your old schoolmates," she mused. "I suppose what's-his-name—Mick—walking out of the flat has to do with the same thing that got Andy all worked up. But you say that one went to work for Solmex and we know the other works for your firm, Trowman. So how come they're both involved?"

"I've got to find out what's been going on." Howell moved out to the centre of the road to see if he could pass the van.

"So's you can go back to your own time and undo it all? I thought you'd given up that notion?"

Lights, a string of them, were coming in the opposite direction. Back in place behind the lorry, he turned to look at her, forehead furrowed, wondering: "What makes you say that?"

"The way you talked after you found out your father was dead," she explained simply. "About you having to go back to your own time knowing just when he was going to die. You talked like you knew then you couldn't do anything to change what was going to happen."

Had he said that? He had, he remembered. And had believed what he was saying. Just as he still firmly believed now that the only possible reason he was being given this sight of his future was because it had to be possible for him to change it once he was back in his own time. Otherwise—and how many times had he reasoned this out?—the whole thing would be pointless.

So here he was, believing two conflicting ideas at the same time. But perhaps they weren't conflicting after all. Perhaps death was different from everything else, in a class by itself, inevitable, too important to be tampered with. That was how it must be. He would be able to change the events leading up to it, but not the manner or time of the event itself. He tried putting all that into words Tina would be able to understand. She grasped it all right, but was very far from convinced, changing the subject abruptly before it developed into an argument again.

"We'll just have to wait and see"—tactfully. And a fresh idea for him to think about: "There is someone else who might be able to help you find out what's been going on, Howie. Anyway, he should at least be able to tell you something about your friend Mick."

There was only the one person he could think of to fit that bill. "You mean Pete, whoever he may be?"

"I liked the look of him. Friendly, like a shaggy pup, you know? And he actually *wanted* to talk to you. Which makes a change. If you don't feel like seeing him yourself, I could do my party piece again. It might be tricky for you, not knowing him from before."

Howell moved out to the middle of the road again. This time it was clear ahead.

"We'll see," he said, suddenly feeling too tired to be bothered about making decisions, only anxious to be home—home!— and in bed.

The car surged forward to pass the endless gleaming length of the biscuit van. The driver put up his hand in a half-salute. With nothing in front of him now, Howell set his foot firmly on the accelerator. A steadily increasing pressure on his upper arm and shoulder was the girl, eyes closed, mouth open a fraction. He let her sleep on, doing his best not to disturb her, not moving his arm even when it became stiff, finding his way back to the suburbs and through the idiot's maze of anonymous side streets without once taking a wrong turning.

He didn't look at the time until he had turned in through

the archway into the deserted, moonlit courtyard and drawn up at the foot of the flight of iron stairs. Quarter to two exactly. He touched the tip of the sleeping girl's nose with his finger. When that didn't rouse her, he shook her arm gently until her eyes opened to gaze blankly up into his. It took her a few seconds to get her bearings.

"Your place?" She sat up. "Well, now"—busy doing things to her hair, patting it back into shape—"you wouldn't have anything special in mind?"

He grinned at her. "Only that I don't much feel like having to find my way back to your dump at this unholy hour of the morning." He opened his door, lowering his voice so as not to wake any of the neighbours. "There's a whole spare room up there, or you can sleep down here in the car. Please yourself."

He climbed out, closed his door quietly and went round to open hers, offering his hand to help her ease herself off her seat.

"And I suppose you're too tired to want to try anything?" she asked in a whisper, on her feet, stretching, pleasant things happening to her white jumper.

"Even with Raquel Welch," he assured her, eyeing those of the neighbouring windows he could see, checking that they had all remained in darkness.

Tina lowered her arms in mock despondency. "Then there's certainly no hope for me."

They tip-toed up the grilled metal steps, Howell with his keys out ready. "Any more *billets-doux*?" Tina looked behind the front door. "No." And nodded in the direction of the kitchen door. "Hot drink before we turn in?"

He liked the idea. "If you're not too tired."

"I am, but who cares?" She called from the kitchen to where he had gone into the long room: "Tea or coffee, take your pick."

"Coffee," he called back, and went into the bedroom that the Howell of now had been using to turn back the bed-clothes and then to sort through the things in the middle one of the dressing table drawers in search of pyjamas. He found the two pairs he was after, one patently fresh from the laundry, the other creased and looking to have been used. Dropping the clean set on the turned-down bed he went into the other bedroom, Mick's room, and dropped the soiled pair on the bed there.

As he returned to the lounge, Tina came through from the kitchen, something in her hand.

"Won't be long, just waiting for the milk to boil. There's a waste-bin in there, under the sink. I had to root through the stuff in it to see if there was anything that might help. I mean, they did overlook that envelope in the cupboard when they went over the joint; they might have missed something else. I found this." She held out a small brown bottle. "It's got your monicker on the label, though, not your friend's. 'H. Trowman,' see? From a chemist." She recited the instructions. "'One capsule to be taken thrice daily, two before retiring.'"

Unscrewing the cap she sniffed delicately at the empty bottle. "I once shared digs with a girl who was on tranquillisers. Nothing drastic, no blue bombers or anything like that. Hers smelt just like this smells now. Not that that means whatever you were on was the same as hers—the smell could be just from the coating. But that 'two before retiring' bit makes it look like they were some kind of tranquillisers."

"Drugs?" He took the bottle from her and put it to his nose. A cloying chocolatey smell. "I've never taken anything like that in my life." But it was his name on the label.

"Everybody takes them these days," Tina informed him extravagantly. "Real fashionable. And yours were probably only very mild. Perhaps you've been overdoing things, overworking. Maybe that's why the doctor wants to see you. He knows you've run out and wants to write you a prescription for some more, before you get too much under the weather."

"Oh"—face turned, nose in the air—"my milk!" And ran back into the kitchen. "It's all right," she called. "I caught it in time."

Howell put the bottle on the sideboard and went to lower himself to the settee. Where Tina shortly joined him, carrying a tray holding two cups of coffee—no saucers—and an opened packet of biscuit—not on a plate.

It seemed she had lost interest in the contents of the bottle, something else having come to occupy her thoughts. And, by her expression, cause her a certain amount of concern.

"In there, I was thinking, Howie—sweet enough for you?" —as he tasted his coffee.

"Fine," he told her. "And what have you been thinking about this time?"

"Ever since walking out of that room this morning—yesterday morning, rather—it's Sunday now—you haven't been to sleep at all, have you? Not even once dozed off for just a few minutes. So you don't know what might happen when you do fall asleep, do you?"

And when, not understanding what she was driving at, he looked perplexed over the rim of his cup: "I mean, for all you know, when you wake up again you may have changed back to the other Howell and will have forgotten all about this, our trip to your home and all the rest of it."

Which was something that hadn't occurred to him. He set his cup down on the floor at his feet, wondering if that was how it would be—to fall asleep here and now, to wake up again in his room back at school in 1969. It was possible, he supposed, but surely what was much more likely, it would happen in exactly the same manner in which he had been brought here—one scene first coming to overlap another, then taking over from it. He would maybe be sitting somewhere, like it was here, he'd look up—no warning or anything—and there would be the window of his room back at school, and that would be it. But that wouldn't happen until he'd found out what he'd been sent here to find.

He smiled reassurance at the girl. "Nothing will happen to me while I'm asleep."

Which is all very well, she thought, judging by her expression. "I don't much fancy the idea of waking up in the morning to find a stranger in the next room," she told him. "Well, almost a stranger, someone I'd met only once before, at a party. And what do you think he'd have to say about finding me in his flat? It doesn't bear thinking about. How can you be so sure it'll be you who'll wake up in the morning?"

"I wasn't sleeping when I was brought here, I was very wide awake. I'll be returned the same way." And then, because he didn't want the thing to develop into a discussion, even an argument, he turned to point to the door of his bedroom. "I've put you in there, Tina. I'll take Mick's room."

The diversion succeeded. "Why your room?"

"The bed in there should have been used regularly," he explained. "The one in Mick's room, if the dust is anything to go by, hasn't been used for some time."

"So it won't be aired. My, aren't we considerate. One thing, I'm used to sleeping raw."

"I've put out a pair of my pyjamas for you."

"Which no doubt will enshroud me like a bell-tent and cover even the tips of my fingers and make me look like something out of the second act of any third-rate bedroom farce. If you've finished your coffee, I'll have your cup."

He took the hint, drained the cup and handed it to her. When she was longer in the kitchen than seemed justified by the washing of only two cups, he went to see what was keeping her. She had found a frying pan and arranged rashers of bacon in it and laid out two eggs alongside. Now she was busy pouring some kind of cereal into two bowls.

"For breakfast," she informed him unnecessarily, seeing him standing there.

"You're very domesticated," he told her for something to say.

She pulled a face. "That's almost as bad as telling a woman she's sensible. You've a lot to learn yet, even though you have caught up with your age." She put the cereal carton in the cupboard. "I suppose I am more domesticated, if that's the word, than most. Comes from having to do for myself from a very tender age. Mom died when I was only eleven, leaving me with two younger sisters and a helpless father to look after. And he was helpless, too, bless him. Always will be. The arty type; clever in his own way. I don't take after him. This was in Chichester. Know it?"

Howell shook his head. "I've never been there."

"Nice little town. We lived just outside. A cottage. I used to think I was stuck there for life. Then he up and married again out of the blue, and for reasons I don't intend going into, I left home. Since then I've drifted from one job to another—maybe I am a bit arty after all. End of saga." She yawned hugely. "I feel almost too tired to sleep." And from the bedroom door: "See you in the morning. And, God, I hope it is you, Howie."

Switching off the lights, he went into Mick's room. A bit on the gaudy side, the creased pyjamas he had tossed on the bed. He wondered whether he had bought them himself, or if they had been a present. Not from Mother—green and purple stripes wouldn't be her choice. Perhaps Aunt Meg, as a change from her everlasting scarfs. But the Aunt Meg of now seemed a very different person from the Aunt Meg of his school days. But waste of time trying to figure out just what could have caused her and Uncle Wilf to change so much, as they obviously had.

And Andy . . . Jacket off, now stripping off his shirt, Howell shook his head at his reflection in the dressing table mirror. If anyone had told him back at school that one day old Andy Brett would look and act like that, he'd have told them not to talk so daft.

Sitting on the side of the bed, he started to remove his shoes and socks. It was odd, now he came to think, how the two people he had last had dealings with in 1969 before all this happened, should be playing such prominent parts in his life now, in 1974. He was actually sharing lodgings with one. And for all the other lived and worked a fairish distance away, there was no doubt from his behaviour that he was very much in the picture. People who haven't met or had anything to do with each other for some time don't go off at the deep end like Andy had.

The three of them had to be linked in some way. A link that had probably existed from the time of them all leaving school. One working for Trowman, the other two for Trowman's biggest rival, Solmex. An odd trio if ever there was one. Bound by the ties of friendship? After the way Andy had acted tonight? That was a laugh. But perhaps they had been friends once. And yet, back at school, Andy and Mick had never been all that close.

Or had they? Howell took off his trousers and hung them over the back of a chair. He had never really taken time out before to think about Andy and Mick in terms of being friends, taking it for granted from the way they acted towards each other when he was with them that there wasn't much they had in common, that they hadn't all that much time for each other.

But, still only a boy, not all that observant, he could have received the wrong impression. They could have been much greater friends than he had ever realised. Their friendship could have persisted until now. And the same thing that had so upset Andy could also have upset Mick, even to the extent of making him feel he could no longer go on sharing lodgings with the cause of that upset. A theory that seemed to fit the few facts he knew. A theory, he recalled, that Tina had already come up with.

Twenty to three, his watch told him as he wound it and put it on the chair he had dragged alongside the bed. The pyjamas felt cold and clammy. After switching off the light he padded over to the window for a final look at the courtyard below, still deserted, still silvered by the moon. Chimney shadows sprawled in eerie fashion. Not even a cat moved. Howell climbed into bed.

He was dreaming. Strangely, he knew all this was a dream and not really happening. But clear and vivid for all that.

He was in the big main office at the Hall, standing at one end, looking along its length to the door at the far end that led to Dad's suite of offices. He had just opened the door of his own office—his name on the glass panel—"Howell Trowman"—no title, no designation—and was standing now in the doorway, waiting for the door of Dad's office to open.

Desks along each side of the room. Clerks, typists, junior secretaries. All the main staff. Faces that he knew and could put names to, all of them. Typewriter keys busily clicking; heads bent over ledgers and folios.

And there was something wrong. He knew that there was something wrong with what was happening, with what was going to happen. He even knew—and this was impossible—what was going to happen. That at any moment that door at the other end of the room would open—

The door opened. Dad was in his shirt sleeves. He always took his jacket off at work. His face, even at the distance, was set in granite-grey lines. He came slowly towards Howell, one hand moving from desk to desk as if steadying himself. Howell went to meet him.

They met, almost as if by arrangement, in the very center of the long room, with all work stopped, machines silent, all heads turned, eyes watching.

And then it came, as he had known it must—Dad's rage, his eyes cold and empty, using the words Howell had known he would use, would have to use, but still shocked, unbelievably shocked by them. All boiling down to the one thing, to the last final burst. "There's nothing more to say. Get out of my sight. I never want to see you again. You are no longer my son."

And to add emphasis, if emphasis were needed, Dad's hand came clamping down hard on his shoulder, gripping painfully, shaking him roughly, shaking—

And still shaking him as the scene melted and changed, as Dad's features blurred and melted and ran. To take on new lines, his cold grey eyes becoming soft brown ones, seeming to be filled with concern, framed by centrally parted straight brown hair.

"Wake up, please," Tina implored, shaking his shoulder and then, as he stared up at her, voicing the concern her eyes were showing. "It is *you*, isn't it, Howie?"

Awake, memory flooding back, he found his voice. "It's me."

"Thank heaven for that." She still shook his shoulder. "You're back with us? You're wanted on the phone. One of the neighbours." She raised her voice, turning to call back over her shoulder: "He's awake. He'll be right along."

A woman's voice called something in return, and there was the sound of a door being slammed. Howell struggled up against the pillows. "Which neighbour? You know which flat?"

"Christ!" It was the first time he had heard Tina use such an expression. "I never thought—" She ran into the lounge. "She's gone. Damn. Now what do we do?" Then: "I know"—and came flying back into the bedroom and over to the window to stand at one side peering out and down, reporting with relief: "Next door but one." And: "Hurry up, Howie!"

He was already out of bed and feeling with his feet for his shoes while he looked in the wardrobe for something to throw over his pyjamas. A raincoat, it had to be. Working his arms into the sleeves as he went, he asked: "Who is it—did she say?"

"No." Hurrying ahead, Tina had the front door open ready. "Only that it's a man." She called after him as he clattered down the tinny steps in unlaced shoes: "Said her name was Nessa something. Bishop, I think."

The courtyard was empty. The iron staircase of the next door but one flat was the same as his. So was the open front door, showing a hall that was a duplicate of his, almost to the furniture. No sign of the woman. He rapped with his knuckles on the open door, bringing the woman from the kitchen. Younger than he had expected, in her thirties; plain, very plain face under short straight black hair cut in an almost pudding-basin fashion with a deep fringe that covered her eyebrows. Her bright red shapeless cotton dress was splattered with what looked like dried blue distemper.

Spoon in one hand, basin in the other, she eyed him as he waited expectantly in the doorway, registering surprise, asking: "So what are you waiting there for?"

"The telephone?" he wondered.

"That's right. I told her, whoever she is. Some man or other. Hadn't you better find out before he rings off?"

"Where is it?"

"Where—?" She stared at him. "What d'you mean—where is it?" She waved the spoon towards the lounge door. "Where it always is, of course. Where it's been for the last five years. What's got into you—not awake yet?—morning after the night before?"

Mumbling something, Howell went into the lounge. A hotch-potch of boxes, furniture, artist's easel, oiled canvases, scattered papers and books. A confusion of overlapping shapes and colours, and an overall smell of curry. He found the telephone, receiver off the hook, behind a pile of magazines on a three-legged table.

A man's voice—oddly hollowed—deep, unnaturally deep and familiar, Howell fancied, for all he couldn't put a name to it.

"Howell Trowman?"

"That's right."

"Listen. I know what you're trying to find out. I can help you if you come to Denver Close, but you must come right away."

A click, and the line went dead.

"Hello?" Howell joggled the cradle automatically, knowing it was waste of time, that whoever it was had rung off.

Replacing the receiver he returned to the hall. From the front door he called: "Thank you." And then paused before calling again: "Do you happen to know where a place called Denver Close is?"

Spoon still in hand, she returned to stand in the kitchen doorway. Before she had been puzzled, perhaps annoyed. Now, by her expression, she was verging on anger.

"If you think I've got time to play games with you—"

There was no point in trying to explain. He thanked her again and made his escape, clattering down one echoing staircase, clattering more slowly up another, to where Tina waited, impatient to hear what the call had been about.

He was able to repeat it to her, word for word, on his way to the bedroom.

Mystified, she followed him to the door. "And that was all—just that?"

"Except that I had the feeling I'd heard the voice before somewhere. God knows where or when." He tossed the raincoat on the bed and started unbuttoning his pyjama jacket. Tina retreated hastily, resuming the conversation out of sight.

"You're going then?"

"I'd be a fool if I didn't." He pulled on his shorts. "Nothing to lose." A wash and a shave would have to wait till he got back.

"Do you know where this Denver Close is, then?"

"No." He slipped his arms into his shirt. "I asked the woman, but she thought—God knows what she thought. Probably that I'm daft. By the way she acted, I must have made a habit of using her phone. And I started off by asking her where the damn' thing was kept."

Slipping on his jacket, not bothering about a tie, he sat on the side of the bed while he did up his shoe laces.

"Decent yet?" Tina called.

"Decent." He stood up. "I'll ask the way from someone outside," he told her, back in the doorway again—fully dressed in her white jumper and black slacks, he noticed for the first time.

"Be careful, Howie," she said as he went past her into the lounge.

The concern in her voice made him stop and turn. "Of what?"

"I don't know. But don't you see, if this man knows you're trying to find out about yourself, then he must know what's happened to you."

"Which makes him one of those mysterious persons who've pumped dope and hypnosis into me," Howell finished for her, and carried on to the front door, stopping there again to shake his head and smile at her. "Nobody has done anything to me, Tina. Not in the way you're thinking, that is."

He went down the iron staircase again. The sun was shining outside—he hadn't had time to notice before. Time . . . He had stuffed his watch in his trouser pocket. He brought it out—twenty past nine—and fastened it on his wrist as he walked past his car and through the archway.

He chose to turn to the right for no other reason than in that direction it was only a few steps to the corner of the street. And reaching that corner he waited for the only person in sight to come up, this an elderly gentleman wearing a black homburg and carrying an elegantly furled umbrella.

"Denver Close?" While the umbrella pointed, china-blue eyes inspected Howell's unshaven chin with mild disapproval. "A stone's throw. The first turning on the right and the first on the left. One of two such closes, the other called Mertyvale Steps, their entrances facing each other. You would be a stranger?"

"Yes," Howell told him.

"Then refuse to be deterred by the unprepossessing approach

—a narrow passage flanked by ugly high walls, a veritable brick-work pass. But once through you will come happily upon one of those small islands of old London left stranded by the surging, relentless tide of progress. Trees, flowers—"

A hobby-horse, clearly, of this old gentleman who looked and spoke as if he himself belonged on one such island. Howell, impatient, broke into his enthusings to thank him before going off in the direction the umbrella had indicated.

An empty quiet street, the first on the right. Quiet indeed, the only sound that of a newspaper boy, canvas bag over shoulder, emerging from one side of the street to cross to the other and vanish out of sight. From right to left, and so, Howell surmised, from Mertyvale Steps into Denver Close.

A "brickwork pass," the man in the black homburg had dramatically called the entrance. "Canyon" would have been a better word. The narrow passage, only wide enough to take one car in comfort, was made dark by the blank brick walls that towered on either side, the end walls of the two flanking four-storey houses. Sunshine flooded beyond, all the more bright for being so framed. An occupant of the close itself, the man on the phone? Or had the place been chosen for its privacy and sense of remoteness?

Howell turned into the shadowy canyon in the wake of the newspaper boy, now almost at the other end. From somewhere behind came the sound of a car engine. But when he glanced back—would the caller come by car?—there was nothing to be seen. And when the sound grew louder, so sure was he that the cause was a car that had just turned into the street leading to the closes and that it would drive straight past the entrances, that he didn't bother to turn around again.

There could be no doubt that the newspaper boy saved his life.

He saw the youth turn, stop and then shout, the words drowned by the engine roar, but their meaning made clear, and a great sense of urgency, by the way the youth gesticulated, pointing, stabbing his finger-pointing hand again and again towards something behind Howell.

And so he turned, to see a black saloon entering the passage behind him, parallel to the walls, and so not just having turned in from the street but coming straight across from the close entrance on the other side. And even then, seeing how it hugged the wall on his side with only inches to spare, coming straight at him—even then, for a fraction of a second, the very last thought in his head was that anyone would want to harm, let alone kill him.

Then realisation of his danger exploded and he turned and was running in the same movement, aware now of nothing else but to reach the end of the passage before the car reached him. The engine roar filled the world, echoing in the confined space, tossed back and to from wall to wall. The corner of the end of the wall on his side had been cut away to make room for a flight of stone steps that seemed to lead nowhere. As he flung himself desperately at them, his fingers scrabbling at the wall, something tugged at the cloth of his trousers and laid heavy numbing pain across his ankle. He stumbled, but remained on his feet on the topmost step, side pressed tight against the wall. The car roared by in a great rush of wind, accelerating, racing into the sunlight, swerving with screaming tyres to avoid the transfixed newspaper boy, roaring across the open space to vanish into the darkness of another passageway beyond.

9

For all the flesh was unbroken, Tina insisted upon first washing the bruise then bandaging it with a clean handkerchief taken from one of the bedrooms. Sitting on the side of the bath, trouser leg rolled to the knee, Howell tried not to wince each time her cool fingers touched that part of his shin where the purple swelling had drawn flesh tightly over bone.

The neighbour with the frizzy black hair and dirty white sweater, the man who had signed himself "Pete" on the note he had pushed under the door, the man they had come back to talk to, seeing in him their last hope of finding out something about Howell's lost years, watched the operation from the bathroom door.

He had been in the lounge when Howell came limping back, sitting contentedly enough in one of the armchairs, managing to give the impression of being a regular visitor to the flat, and that his usual chair. And he was there, as he explained briefly to Howell, because: "Like I told your chick here, Nessa thought I ought to come and see what's going on. She says you acted kinda queer when you came to take that call, like you was dazed, like you was really way out. She thought maybe something had happened." And, looking at Howell's ankle: "Something has, by the looks of it."

Surprisingly, Tina hadn't needed any persuading that the episode in the Denver Close passage had been no accident. "I did warn you to be careful, Howie," she reminded him, preoccupied, more concerned at that moment about treating the injury than discussing how it had been caused.

It appeared that the neighbour had been put in the picture. While waiting for Howell to return, Tina had taken it upon herself to tell him the whole story.

Howell looked up from watching the finishing touch of a strip of adhesive tape being applied to the bandage to examine for the first time the not over-clean, arty-looking individual who lounged in the bathroom doorway. His expression was hard to read. There was disbelief there—some at least, Howell felt, and that was natural enough. But allied with it was what seemed to him a kind of humorous indulgence. Pete smiled a little under the inspection, smiled sideways and nodded, by his attitude not intending to be the one to open any conversation.

"I've either made the whole thing up or else I'm out of my mind," Howell said.

"You didn't make that up, anyway," Pete said drily, nodding at the injured ankle. "And your chick, who doesn't seem to me to be missing any of her marbles, doesn't seem to think you're short of any of yours either."

"We do know each other, you and I?" Howell asked.

"We do," the other agreed, this time managing to give the impression of taking part in a charade.

"I don't expect you to believe the truth," Howell said steadily. "I can't expect anyone to believe anything so impossible. I'm not particularly concerned one way or another. But if we know each other, then you must know something about me, and that's what I want to find out."

For the first time, Pete seemed to be nonplussed, his vaguely supercilious smile tending to become fixed. He looked from Howell's face into the girl's preoccupied one.

"Man, it's wild," he said almost defensively. "That story of yours. Even though your chick here told it to me without batting an eye, as if she meant every word of it. You've got to admit it's way, way out." He scratched at the curly black peninsula of hair that decorated his forehead. "You've been shot here from—when?—five years ago, she says, and you're here just to find out what's been happening, and when you've found out, you'll be shot right back. Man. That's what you believe, so she says. And she believes you've been got at, tampered with, mucked about, just to make you believe what you do believe, and that's almost as wild. Nothing much to choose between the two of them. That"—nodding at Howell's leg—"is real enough, anyway. That's not way out. And you say it wasn't an accident?"

"It was deliberate," Howell replied patiently. "I wasn't the only one to think that."

"You weren't? Oh, you mean the kid that warned you."

"It took me some time to persuade him into thinking it must have been an accident after all."

The other was puzzled. "And why did he have to be persuaded?"

"The odds are he'll tell his parents about it," Howell explained simply. "And it might get from them to the police."

Pete's expression changed. "The police? And why don't you want them to know?"

"Because—" Howell started wearily, then caught Tina's eye and gestured, leaving the explaining to her.

"I told you that Howell thinks he's only here for a short time," she told Pete. "He doesn't want to waste any more of that time than he can help. That's why he hasn't felt like talking to people, because he's afraid they'll think he's sick, lost his memory, and call in a doctor. He took a chance on looking up one of his old school friends, but all he got was black looks and a door slammed in his face. We came back here because the only other person we could think of who might help was you."

Pete nodded slowly, his eyes on her face. "That'll be because of that note I shoved under the door. I felt pretty sure there was somebody home."

"At least you still seemed to be speaking to him, which is more than you can say of his friend out at Gretton." Tina straightened, finally satisfied she had done all she could to make Howell's leg more comfortable. "What did the doctor want to see him about—Mr. Bishop, isn't it? I think that was the name your wife said."

"The doc—" Pete came out of a small reverie. "Oh, he didn't say. Only that he wanted to see Mr. Trowman as soon as possible, and if I saw him, would I pass the message on. And my name's not Bishop. Nessa's the Bishop. I'm Foster, Peter Foster. We aren't married, we just shack up together. Convenient all along the line. I paint for a living. Paint—" He sneered at himself. "Anything from souvenir ashtrays to snotty-nosed dwarfs on Christmas price tags. And when—"

He broke off, leaning forward to stare closely at Howell's face. Where a flush had come, only a faint pinkness, but undeniably a flush, brought there by Pete's disclosure of his domestic arrangements.

"He's still a little of each," Tina said, talking of Howell as if he weren't there. "At first, when he first came to see me, he was still a schoolboy—seventeen, but acting younger than that. Then when he heard about his father being dead he grew up in a few minutes. Now he seems to be a bit of each, you know?"

"I'm damned," Pete said softly, marvelling. "I thought—hell, it doesn't matter what I thought. But I wasn't going to be taken in. I'll string along, I thought. Maybe he's a better actor than I'd ever given him credit for, I thought. But lying to high heaven—he had to be. Taken you in, and thinking I'll be just as easy, and anyone else who cares to listen. Not me, I thought. So he's worked out a real good yarn and learnt how to lie and keep a straight face. But I've never heard tell of anyone able to make themselves get all red in the face to order. Maybe it's possible. I dunno. But it looks like he really did get all hot under the collar about me and Nessa shacking up without church bells."

He looked down at Howell's ankle again.

"That's for real, anyway. And it happened in Denver Close like he said. So far as I know he's never been up that way before, so he couldn't have known about those steps he managed to reach just in time. They're an old horse-mounting block. Only a few of them left around now. So I'll go along when he says it was deliberate. And in broad daylight—"

Pete looked up again. "I never thought of that before. Whoever it was tried to rub him out, took the risk of doing it in broad daylight instead of waiting for darkness, when there'd have been no risk at all. Well, maybe there are cranks knocking round who'd like to get at him for what they think he did, but after all these weeks, why the sudden hurry? Why did it have to be this morning when tonight would have been so much better?

"What do we know about the call? I was out when it came, getting my Sunday paper. A man, Nessa says, and speaking from a call box."

"There's one just round the corner," Tina supplied.

"So there is." Forehead creased in concentration, Pete thrust his clenched fists up and under his thick once-white pullover to give himself knuckled breasts. "He drives to Mertyvale Steps—that's just across from where you nearly copped it, Howell—parks just out of sight, walks back to the box—only a couple of minutes—to make the call, then goes back to sit in his car to wait for you to show up. As simple as can be. What about the car?"

Howell finally rolled down his trouser leg and slid off the side of the bath to test his weight gingerly on an ankle that had started to stiffen up.

"Black," he grunted, "a black saloon. That's all I know."

Pete didn't believe him. "You must've seen more than that. What about the driver? What about the registration?"

"It was all over in seconds." Howell edged by Pete into the lounge and limped to the settee to sit down with his leg stretched out in front. "The driver was just a blur. I didn't even see any number plates."

"What about the voice, then?" Pete followed him into the room, seating himself in his original armchair. "A man, Nessa says. I could talk to her, ask her if she recognised it at all."

"The fewer people who know, the better," Howell said. "In any case, I'm almost certain it was disguised."

"Handkerchief over mouthpiece—that sort of thing?" Pete's

eyes gleamed. "All the trimmings. Could it have been a woman by any chance?"

Howell considered that possibility. "I suppose so," he said doubtfully.

"Can you remember now what this he or she had to say?"

"Not the exact words." Howell stooped to massage the top of his foot. "Something about knowing what it was I was trying to find out, and that he could help me but only if I went straight away to Denver Close."

"And according to your chick here, the only thing you're trying to find out is what's been going on over the past five years."

"And for the caller to know that," Tina inserted, "means he must know something's been done to Howie to make him lose that part of his memory. And if he knows that, then I say he must be one of the people who actually did it."

"Logical," Pete agreed. "I suppose so, anyway." He turned back to Howell. "So the moment you get the message you drop everything and go belting off without even stopping to think."

"I had the feeling something was wrong," Tina supplied. "I did warn him to be careful."

"No matter what anybody else thinks or believes," Howell said heavily, "I know that I've been sent here to find out what I've done with my life the last five years. The man said he could help me. That was good enough for me. With even one of my best friends turned against me I couldn't afford to let the chance slip by. And there was no reason I knew of why anyone should want to harm me in any way, let alone try to kill me."

"What you think has happened to you," Pete stated flatly, "couldn't have happened. You just can't get shifted from one year to another like pieces on a chess board. That's out. Neither do I go along with what your chick thinks happened. That's almost as far out as your version. I have my own idea of what it's all about, and I'm taking bets on long odds that I'm not far off the truth. You wanna know? I'll tell you. Things got on top of you—not surprisingly—you finally cracked and lost a whole slab of that part of your memory you'd much rather forget anyway. And then your subconscious or whatever came up with an explanation to cover the loss. How does that strike you both?"

Howell leaned back. "If it's the way you think—" he started.

And then Tina broke in: "I've just thought of something." And when they both turned to look at her: "Whoever it was tried to kill Howie must know you, Pete. Otherwise he wouldn't have known where to ring to get hold of Howie, don't you see? He must have known you were a neighbour of his in the habit of taking phone calls for him."

Pete remained unimpressed by her reasoning. "You've not mentioned anything about having been out of the country," he observed drily, "so I'm guessing you're not a great one for reading newspapers."

"I read them the same as everyone else," she told him distantly.

"You mean you just skim through them. If you read them properly you couldn't help but know something of what happened in our little neck of the woods here. I reckon a few million people must have read about my phone being used by Howell Trowman and Martin Debroy."

"The papers—" Tina turned to Howell. "That man at the pub—remember?—he went on about reporters when I asked him about you. We said then there must have been something about you in the papers, something pretty big." She swung excitedly back to Pete to demand: "What was it all about?"

Scratching again at his forehead tuft, he seemed in no great hurry to tell them. "It was headlines—you must have read something. You couldn't have missed it."

"I had the feeling I'd come across the name Debroy somewhere before," she replied impatiently.

"Yeah." He eyed each of them in turn. "I still don't know what to make of all this. It doesn't seem to be an act the pair of you are putting on, some sort of brain-storm lost memory gag to work back into an alibi or something, with me the first one to be taken in by it so that I can stand up in court if needs be and swear to high heaven that you really have got something weird going on inside your head and that your memory's gone for a burton. You both seem genuine enough, but I'm still not so sure. Look—"

He leaned forward, eyes narrowed, his pointed finger swivelling between the girl's face—a blend of impatience and rising indignation—and Howell's relatively placid features.

"You, the pair of you, you say all this started sometime yesterday, and all you've done since then is try to fill in that five-year gap. All right, so just how much have you got?"

"Not that much," Howell replied evenly. By now he had a good idea of the kind of person Pete was—stubborn, possessed of a great sense of his own importance, an inferiority complex, afraid of being taken in, of having his ego dented. The only way to deal with a man like that was letting him know you didn't expect him to accept anything at face value.

He listed the few items as they came to mind. "I've found out that my father's dead, that I don't work for his firm but I'm employed by one of its rivals. I seem to have done something to turn quite a few people against me and get my name in the papers. I share this flat with an old school friend of mine called Mick Debroy—his name's actually Martin. And we think, by the look of his room, that he hasn't used it for some time."

Tina added, when it seemed Howell wasn't going to include it in his list: "And it's obvious that somebody has been all through the place taking away anything that might have told Howie the name of the person sharing the flat with him. I say it must be the same people who've done something to his mind."

"But you still managed to find out it was Debroy," Pete said. "I wondered why neither of you said anything when I mentioned his name. And how did you manage to find out it was him if there's nothing of his left here?"

Tina explained about the old envelope she had found in the kitchen cupboard. Looking vaguely disappointed, as if he had hoped he had caught them out, Pete nodded. "As simple as that." And then, suddenly: "Have you come across a brief case in your travels?"

Their faces told him they had. And that it wasn't just any old brief case.

He rubbed the side of his thick nose. "So it's still here."

"What do you know about it?" Howell asked warily.

"Not very much. I don't know what's in it, if that's what you're wondering. By the look on your faces, you pair do, though."

"It wasn't locked when we found it," Howell said, trying to sound matter-of-fact, as if there hadn't been anything important or of value in it.

"It was when you gave it to me to keep for you that time," Pete said drily. "I tried all my keys to see if any fitted. Curiosity always was one of my failings."

He was clearly inviting now to be told what the brief case contained. But for all the small outward display of being honest—honest enough to admit to having tried to open the case himself, there was something about him—with his frizzy black hair, open-ugly face and thick-lipped smile that Howell didn't all that much care for. And so, like the girl, he remained silent.

There was a short, uncomfortable hiatus. Then Pete made quite a thing of first laboriously crossing one leg over the other, then tugging down the front of his chunky, dirty pullover over the beginnings of a middle-aged stomach, finally addressing himself to his paint-splattered right shoe.

"For better or worse I'm going to go along with you. For the time being, anyway. Until either of you drop a clanger. And if all this is some sort of gag you've cooked up between you, to make use of me or anyone else you can rope in, then sooner or later one of you is going to drop one.

"You were right when you said someone had been through the flat taking away everything with Debroy's name on it. But it wasn't anyone outside the law, like you"—looking at Tina—"seem to think. It was the law itself, the police, and they were after anything that might have given them a lead."

He went on quickly, not giving them a chance to interrupt.

"And you were right again when you guessed by the state of Debroy's room that he hadn't used it for some time. Nearly

119

two months, it would be. I had to think. More like two years, it seems."

He looked at Howell.

"That was the night you found his body down below in your garage. Murdered—head smashed in. And with everything pointing to you being the one who'd done it. So that everyone's wondering now why you haven't been arrested, why you're still running around loose."

10

IT WAS POSSIBLE, HOWELL THOUGHT, that Pete had delivered the blow so abruptly, no holds barred, in almost violent terms, for no other reason than, containing a streak of sadism, he liked to watch the suffering of others. Or it could be he had hoped to shock his victim into some kind of give-away reaction. Or again, it would be more charitable to assume he had simply wanted to get the telling of such news over and done with as quickly as possible.

Whichever it was, Howell was conscious of no great sense of shock. Andy Brett's behaviour had been more than enough to convince him that the Howell of now must be mixed up in something particularly unsavoury. That that something was murder, with himself the suspected murderer, left him virtually unmoved. Not because his mind had been numbed by the news but simply because it had nothing to do with him, didn't concern him—at least at that moment—in any way. He was nothing more than an observer. What had happened in the garage two months ago belonged to the future. So far as he was concerned it hadn't happened yet, wouldn't for another five years, might not even happen at all.

And another thought . . . One kind of death—the natural death of his father—was irrevocable. But the other kind—unnatural and violent—might be a very different matter.

"You don't seem all that put out," Pete said suspiciously. "For someone who's not supposed to know what's been going on and who's just been told he's suspected of having done in his flat-mate, you're taking it very calmly."

He turned to look at the girl, white-faced, holding on to the arm of the settee for support.

"You didn't know, anyway," he added drily. "You all right?"

Tina nodded and found her voice. "I will be." She dropped heavily on to the other side of the settee from Howell, jerking his leg, making him wince.

Missing his expression of pain, she leaned across to put her hand on his arm. "You didn't do it, Howie. You couldn't have, you're not that sort, nor the you you're going to be, so don't get thinking he did." She laughed shakily, the colour starting to return to her cheeks. "Sort that out."

Pete had done. "You're very trusting," he said, in no way sneering.

"I've not known him all that long, but long enough to know he couldn't do a thing like that."

"Me, I've been his neighbour for a couple of years," Pete told her. "Not that we ever got what you might call intimate. Kept himself pretty much to himself. Could be you've got to know him better in a few hours than I did in all that time."

"You don't think he did it either," she reasoned, completely herself again now. "Otherwise you wouldn't have been concerned enough about him to have come round here to find out if he was all right when your—when Nessa told you he'd been acting odd."

"Could have been curiosity." He grinned sideways. "On the other hand you could be right."

She leaned forward. "Why do they think he did it?"

Pete shrugged. "Because they can't think of anyone else who could have done it. His is the only name on the list. According to the fuzz, Marty had no enemies at all and hardly any friends. There was no reason why anyone should have wanted to do him in. So all they could do was guess. And Howell was the only one they could guess about. There was a girl. Janet something. Janet Howle. Not bad if you like the slinky hippy type.

Both Marty and Howell had her out at different times. Some papers said they must have quarrelled over her. Others said it was all to do with Howell being jealous over Marty getting on better at work, making more bread. Weak, that one. Other guesses, too—I forget now. I do remember one rag writing about means, motive and opportunity, and saying he had the means—a heavy car spanner, it was—and the opportunity—late at night in the garage where nobody could hear anything. All that was missing was the motive, and that was the only reason the fuzz hadn't nabbed him. They're probably still looking. That's why they took all Marty's personal stuff away from the flat, of course. Anything they thought might give them a lead." He paused significantly. "Seemingly all except for one thing. That's if it was his. It didn't have his name or initials on it, anyway."

"The brief case," Howell said.

"Yeah, that." Pete made a face. "I kept mum about it when they came nosing round. By rights I should have told. Maybe it's evidence, maybe not."

More than evidence, Howell thought, a motive.

"Why didn't you tell the police about it?" he asked steadily enough.

"Now you're asking me." Pete moved his chunky shoulders. "Maybe because it's not done to help the fuzz. Or maybe like your chick here I didn't think you was the one who'd done it, and telling about the brief case might have laid the finger right on you. I figured there had to be a good reason why you asked me to take care of it till the fuzz had done sniffing around."

"When did all this happen?" Howell asked.

"Not quite two months ago. A Friday, May twenty-fourth. A real stinker of a night, raining and windy. About half eleven it must've been when you came knocking on our door. Nessa was in bed, I was just finishing a job for a local shop. Man, were you in a state . . . Like you'd had a bummer and a half. Like you was spaced-out. I knew you were under the doc and on some sort of dope. You was like you was sleep-walking. You said you'd just got back, opened the garage to put your car away, and there was Marty Debroy lying on the floor with blood on his head. You said that was how you'd come by the blood on your hands. I hadn't noticed it till then. You had the brief case under your arm. Marty was dead, you said, and could you use our phone to call the police, and would I look after your brief case until after they'd been and gone. I reckon I must've been so shook up I said yes without even thinking what I was saying yes to. You asked for it back about a fortnight later."

"I see." Absently rubbing his ankle, Howell stared at the opposite wall. Another piece had been fitted into the picture of the future. Another very important piece was still missing.

"How long is it since my father threw me out of the firm?" he asked.

Pete shook his head. "One thing you never talked about was your folks."

"You're guessing that that's what must have happened, Howie?" Tina asked.

"It's more than a guess." He told her about the dream. "A bit of the other Howell must have come through, some of his memories. It was so vivid I think it must have been exactly the way it was in the dream."

"His dream, not yours." Pete grimaced. "Weird. No, the first mention I'd heard of your old man was when you said a while back that one of the things you'd been able to find out was that he had died, by the sound of it in the last five years. He was in business?"

"Trowman Chemicals," Howell said shortly, and the other gaped at him.

"You're not *that* Trowman?"—incredulously, and turned his disbelief on the girl. And when she nodded: "Jesus . . . Man, but they're big, I mean, really big. But how come you and Marty worked for Solmex?"

"That's one of the things I was hoping you would be able to tell me," Howell said.

"I'm sorry." Over his surprise, Pete leaned back again. "I'll tell you everything I know about you, and it isn't very much. Me and Nessa came here about five years back. Your friend Marty Debroy moved in about a month after, but you didn't show up till about two years ago. The autumn of 'seventy-two.

124

September. You didn't bring much stuff with you. Your car was the same old banger you got parked out front now. Marty used to change his car about once a year, but you stuck to the same old one. Like you didn't have the bread to throw round like him. You and him seemed to get on all right—not soul-mates, just buddy-buddy. The fuzz said he hadn't any enemies and very few friends. I reckon they could have said the same about you. So far as me and Nessa knew, anyway. Anything else I can tell you?"

He seemed ready now to help as much as he could.

"You'd been under the weather. Have I said that? Not sick, like. Nerves. Like when you're in the rat race. Overwork, tension, all that jazz. You were under the doc and on some sort of dope. Then you had a blackout, at least one, maybe more. I can't think of anything else worth mentioning."

Howell tried prompting him. "Have you ever heard me say whether or not I went to a university?"

Pete thought. "Not that I recollect."

Howell tried again. "If it was five years ago when Mick first came here, he must have come straight from school."

"He was young all right." The other grinned at memories. "Little more than a kid. And looking pretty well down on his uppers when he first came. Real tatty, the stuff he brought with him. Started to blossom out about a year later. Shove-up at his work, I guess."

Howell couldn't think of anything else to ask at that moment. In the hiatus Tina discovered with some dismay that it was quarter to eleven. "And we haven't even had breakfast yet." She sped to the kitchen.

"And I suppose I'd better be getting back to my pad," Pete offered with no great enthusiasm.

But: "Coffee?" she called back, and, going through the motions of collecting his strength for the big job of pushing himself up out of his chair, he collapsed back again with a gusty sigh of relief.

He met Howell's eye. "If I'm in the way, just say. Only I don't want to miss any of this." He scratched at the curly frontal peak of his hair, seemingly a favourite gesture of his when unsure of himself. "I still don't know what to make of it all. Your chick's idea doesn't hold water, anyway. About the flat having been gone over by the same crowd that fixed you or whatever. Like I said, it was the fuzz who searched the place. So that only leaves your version. And man, is that wild. But someone tried to rub you out—I'll buy that part of it."

"The same person who killed his friend," Tina supplied knowledgeably from the kitchen door.

"Could be. But don't forget Marty was done in a couple of months back. Why wait till now before having a go at Howell, and then be in such a hurry all at once they can't even wait for it to get dark?"

"I don't know," she said. "How d'you like your coffee?"

"Black." He turned back to Howell. "Any use asking if you know of any reason why anyone should want to rub you and Marty out?"

"You know as much as I do of what I've been doing these last five years."

"Yeah. I figured that what little I was able to tell you couldn't have helped very much. Except about you being mixed up in a murder. At least you know the worst that could have happened to you."

Howell leaned back against the cushions. "I don't think that is the worst," he said slowly. "I don't think Andy Brett would have turned against me the way he has just because some people seem to think I murdered Mick Debroy. I think there's something else."

"Worse than murder . . ." Pete whistled softly. "Brett . . . He's the one you went out to the country to see?"

"Gretton." Howell nodded. "He wouldn't even give me a chance to tell him what had happened."

"I think you ought to try him again," Pete said.

Sensible enough advice. But it would just be a waste of time.

"*Make* him listen to you," Pete urged.

Grab him when he opens the door, pin him against the wall, yell at him?

"Tell you what," Pete said. "Let me talk to him on the blower. Surely he'll listen to me. Let me tell him enough of what you say's happened to get him interested. How does that grab you?"

"He can at least try," Tina said from the kitchen door.

It might work. "I don't even know if his digs are on the phone," Howell said. "He's staying with people called—" He had forgotten the name.

Tina hadn't. "Humphrey. And the number of the house is twenty-three. I don't know the name of the road."

"Gretton Lane," Howell supplied. "And it's the Ascot exchange."

"If they're on the phone, I'll get them." Pete pushed himself to his feet and then waited, expecting Howell to do the same.

But Howell had other ideas. "If you can get him to listen to you and agree to talk to me, tell him I'll come down to Gretton again. There's too much to discuss over the phone."

"Just as you say." Pete sounded disappointed. "What about that coffee?" he asked Tina.

"It'll be ready by the time you get back," she promised.

"Like I gotta earn it first." Pete lumbered like a bear through the hall door. They heard his heavy footsteps on the iron staircase outside.

"I like him," Tina said. "In a way I feel sorry for him, you know? Trying to sound like he's still with it, and he's not, he was left behind years ago."

"Like some of the RAF types of my time," Howell said, understanding. "Many of them still clinging to their ridiculous moustaches and the expressions that went with them."

"They're still with us," she told him. "We're only five years ahead of you, not twenty-five." She returned to her stove.

A few seconds later Howell caught the sound of a car door being slammed somewhere outside. He limped into his bedroom to peer cautiously from the window. The large black saloon, drawn up just behind his own small car, and turned round ready for leaving again, he recognised immediately. And one of the men who had just emerged from it—still bare-headed, wearing the same loose coat as yesterday. Doctor Wharton. Slim and professional-looking, and very different from his companion, the man now easing himself out of the back of the car, awkwardly by virtue of his bulk—a huge, gross hulk of a man, the material of his blue suit looking to be strained to bursting point across his massive shoulders, stomach and thighs. He was almost bald, the shining white dome of his head encircled by a wispy monkish tonsure of grey. His face—even from the distance—was small and grotesquely babylike, like an evil puppet —features collected together and dwarfed by the surrounding mass of wax-white flesh. A caricature of a man. An unforgettable man. And Howell, staring down at him, had the feeling he had seen him somewhere before. Talking together, the doctor glancing up at the windows—Howell drew back—the two men made their way towards the iron staircase.

In the kitchen, Tina was singing softly to herself. Howell hushed her from the doorway, one hand asking silence, the other pointing in the direction of the front door. She understood, nodding, even turning out the gas under her spluttering frying pan, mouthing silently: "Who is it?"

He shook his head. Three taps came to the front door, a short interval, then three more, louder. Then voices, the words indistinguishable, the sound receding as the two men climbed back down to the courtyard.

"It was the doctor again," Howell explained over his shoulder on his way back to the window.

Tina followed him to peep over his shoulder, fretting, worried, wondering: "Should we have seen him, do you think? It must be something important for him to have come again and on a Sunday." And then, as the two reappeared below: "Who's that monster with him?"

"I don't know." He frowned. "I think I've seen him before, but I can't remember where."

She shuddered. "Once seen, never forgotten. Isn't he an awful-looking man? If you have seen him before it could only have been for a moment, otherwise you wouldn't have forgotten."

The two climbed back into their car, the vehicle canting over under the weight of the big man. Pete came into view as it moved away to swing through the archway. He stood for a moment looking after it before turning towards the stairs.

Tina returned to the kitchen by way of the hall, going the long way round so that she could open the front door ready for Pete. Howell rested his hands on the cold glass of the window, racking his brain, coming up with nothing for his pains other than the vague impression that the big man was to do with now, not the past. Perhaps he had seen him in the street somewhere—a passing glimpse would be more than enough for such a giant to stick in the memory.

"Was that Wharton I just saw driving off?" Pete asked from the doorway behind.

Howell turned to nod and anticipate the next question. "I didn't open the door."

"I figured you hadn't. You know best. In your place I think I'd want to know what he's so keen to see me about. And who was that with him, for Gawd's sake? I caught sight of him as he got back in the car. Man, he's a big one. D'you know who it was?"

"I was hoping you might have been able to tell me."

"No playmate of mine." Pete grinned. "I like 'em more my own size. Right. About your pal out at Gretton. Man, you've got a right obstinate bastard there. All right till I told him I was a friend of yours, and then man, that was it. Like I never even got a chance to get started. Like whammo, curtains, finito. Like he slammed the receiver down like he had a grievance against my eardrum."

"I thought it might be like that," Howell said, only slightly disappointed. He had had very little hope of the attempt succeeding.

"Yeah. Whatever it is you've been up to, you've sure got that one riled. So what do you do now?"

"Coffee," Tina called.

"No luck with Andy," Howell told her in the lounge.

"I know, I heard." She didn't seem too concerned. "Will you have your breakfast in the lounge or the kitchen?"

He chose the kitchen to save her the trouble of carrying the things through. Pete followed to sit astride a stool dragged from the recess under the draining-board, cradling his cup in stubby, paint-stained fingers.

Howell was still trying to remember where he could possibly have seen the big man before. More than a vague feeling now— a certainty. Or could it be another memory that had leaked through from the Howell of now?

"Is Wharton your doctor?" he asked Pete through a mouthful of bacon.

"No." Pete derided the idea. "We don't have one, not even on anyone's list. Me and Nessa don't have time to get sick."

"How do you know him then?"

The other frowned a little at the question. "Through him coming here to see you—what did you think?"

"I thought doctors didn't pay visits to patients with only nervous troubles. They expect the patients to go to them."

"Not when the patients have blackouts. Like the one you had that time. Marty managed to get you to bed, then came belting round to us to call the doc. I came back here with him and I was still here when Wharton showed up." Pete's frown deepened. "What do you think you're on to now?"

"We have no way of telling if he's a doctor at all," Howell said evenly.

Pete set down his cup with exaggerated care. "And what, for Gawd's sake, put that idea in your head? Because you think you've seen the geezer who was with him before?"

Which was certainly one of the reasons why Howell had doubts about Wharton. There was another.

"How long will it be since I had that blackout and he came here to see me?"

Pete had to think. "It would be about two months before Marty got done in. That makes it four months altogether."

"And he hasn't been here since?"

Pete picked up his cup again. "Not that I know of."

"Yet now he's been here twice within the last twenty-four hours."

"I see what you're getting at." The other stared down into his cup. "Why this sudden interest in you?" He looked up. "Unless he knows something odd's happened to you."

"He couldn't. The only people I've talked to, the only people who can possibly know, are you and Tina."

130

Hovering in the background, Tina thought of something.

"He *is* a doctor, Howie. I looked him up in the phone book, remember?"

Howell helped himself to the last piece of toast. Not particularly hungry when he started eating, now he was enjoying the meal.

"Just because there's a Dr. Wharton in the book doesn't mean he was the man who came here," he pointed out, and turned back to Pete to ask: "Have you ever been to his surgery? Have you ever seen him visiting anyone else?"

"No to both." Pete pored over his empty cup, absently waving aside Tina's pantomimic offer of more coffee. "It was Marty who first sent for him. When he came he had his little black bag and all the trimmings. He looked like a doctor, smelt like one, talked like one, went through all the motions. But I've never seen him in his surgery, and I've never seen his diploma."

He looked up. "I tell you what I can do, though. I can go back to my pad and ring him up and if it is him, and he's genuine, I can always use the excuse I'm calling for you to find out what he wants to see you about. Kill two birds with one stone. How does that grab you?"

Howell pushed his empty plate aside and picked up his cup. "It's an idea," he said expressionlessly.

"Okay." Pete slid to the floor, deposited his empty cup in the sink—"That was coffee, Tina mia; I'll have to send my woman round to you for lessons"—and lumbered out.

Howell stopped drinking to watch him go. Tina, starting to clear the table, studied his face. "You don't like him, do you, Howie? Why not?"

"I don't know." His dislike was unfounded, he knew that—a groundless, instinctive emotion. And because of the dislike there was also distrust. So that if Pete were to report that Wharton was genuine, he wouldn't know whether to believe him or not.

"You don't really think he can have anything to do with what's been done to you?" Tina asked.

"I don't know what to think. I suppose I'm getting to the

stage of being afraid to trust anybody. Someone's had one try at killing me, could be they'll try again."

No "could be" about it, he thought. As sure as God made little apples they'll try again.

"What about me?" she wanted to know. "Mata Hari, or still the little girl guide?"

He grinned at her, throwing a two-fingered salute. "If you were on their side you could have helped dispose of me last night when I was asleep."

"That's a happy thought." At the sink she turned on the tap to fill a kettle. "Look, I've got to go out this afternoon. If you like, I could try to find out about Wharton for you, that's if it'll make you any easier in your mind."

Startled, he ignored the offer. "What do you have to go out for?"

She smiled, obviously pleased at his concern. "I've got to go to my place, of course. I brought nothing with me when I left yesterday, you know that. I wasn't expecting to stay the night. I want to change my clothes, clean my teeth properly, brush my hair, put on fresh make-up, oh—dozens of things. And I've got to go anyway to see if there's a message for me. Sometimes they ask me to work on a Sunday evening. Not very often, but I'm supposed to be on tap if they do. And I'm going to get out of turning in tomorrow morning. That's if you think you'll still be here and needing my valuable assistance."

"I have the feeling I'll still be here. And I'd be lost without you."

"That's nice." She patted his cheek, pleased again, this time at his obvious sincerity, at the warmth of his tone.

"Who do you work for?" he asked awkwardly.

"I told you, a welfare organisation." The kettle boiled and she turned out the gas and poured the water into the sink. "You can dry; there's the towel."

He took it down from its hook behind the hall door. The front door, he noticed, had been left open.

"What's your lot called?" he asked, back at her side.

"You'd only laugh if I told you."

"I won't." He looked for somewhere to put the dried dishes.

132

"Angels Anonymous," she said reluctantly. And: "I knew you'd laugh."

"I was just wondering where you keep your wings when you're off duty."

"We've heard it all before," she told him resignedly. "From Come fly with me to Is that your halo on the hat rack?"

It was the first time he had really laughed since arriving in 1974. He felt better for it. Recovering—"I'll drive you to your place."

"Thanks, but I'll manage fine with underground and bus. It's better you stay here in case Pete or anyone else tries to get in touch. You won't find out anything about your lost five years driving me back and to across London."

Which was true enough. "At least let me pay for a taxi."

"You'll do no such thing." She had second thoughts. "I don't know, though. I forgot about all that money. Howie—" Turning to him she laid her wet hand on his arm. "If the police knew about what's in that brief case, they might say it was a motive, mightn't they?"

But before he could reply—

"Here we are," Pete announced brightly from the hall doorway. "Back to report. Not that I've had much success. Wharton's part of a group practice—you know the racket—three doctors sharing the same surgery. Being Sunday, only one of 'em's on call, a geezer called Griffin. He did his best to help, though. But he'd never heard of you, Howell, he didn't know where Wharton could be reached and he couldn't find a card for you in the file. Which, he said, probably means Wharton has it with him. And that's all."

He made no move to come further into the kitchen. "Except that my female reminded me there's a job I have to have ready by tomorrow morning and that it was high time I got down to it. Incidentally, I haven't said anything to her about all this; she'd never believe it, anyway. I'll look in from time to time. Anything else you want me for, you know where to find me. Be seeing you."

"Suddenly he finds urgent work," Howell said when Pete had gone. "An excuse to get away?"

"Now, why should he want to get away, and why should he need an excuse?" Tina shook her head at him. "Just because you've taken a dislike to him."

He turned from hanging up the towel. "I think he heard us talking about the brief case."

"If he had, he'd have said something." Rooting round, she had found a duster and a hand brush. "I'll give the place a rough going-over before I start getting lunch ready. You go in the other room and make yourself scarce."

In the lounge he stretched out on the settee, looking up at the wire-mesh-covered skylights, the glass yellow and streaked with city grime. His ankle felt much easier, more stiff than painful now.

He didn't see how Pete could have avoided overhearing Tina's mention of the brief case and its contents. And now would he go straight to the police? Was that why he had been in such a hurry to leave? But he had kept quiet about it once before—if his story was to be believed—when by so doing he was suppressing evidence and possibly implicating himself in murder. If he had thought about it, he had as good as said, he wouldn't have taken in the brief case. Would the police accept that excuse if he told them about it now?

Howell closed his eyes. The grey behind his closed lids turned to purple, after a while became the black emptiness of limitless space. Far away was a pin-prick point of light. He was rushing towards it, or it towards him. It grew larger as it came nearer. Shape came to it—oval and irregular, and with more brightness towards the top. And patterned, an irregular pattern centred on four focal points. Four points that resolved themselves into two eyes, a nose and a mouth. A face that was unnatural and grotesque. A baby face set in waxen plumpness beneath a glistening hair-fringed dome. A face he recognised, that was frightening and yet brought no sense of fear. It came hurtling towards him, expanding, pushing aside the velvet blackness, filling the universe behind his closed eyes, powerful, trying to suck him into itself, reaching out with invisible hands—

Tina's hand on his shoulder brought him awake. Lunch was ready. Bacon again, beans and some kind of thick pancake fried in the bacon fat. A fruit pie that she cut in the box in which it had come. There was even some cheese.

He didn't tell her about the dream. From his memory had it come? Or from that of the Howell of now?

They took their coffee through to the lounge. "Fifteen minutes," she warned, "that's all. It's getting on for three o'clock, and it'll take me the best part of an hour to get home."

He helped her clear the table and wash the dishes. It was half past three by the time they had finished. She washed her face, combed her hair and was ready to leave. He wanted her to take two of the five-pound notes—"Just to be on the safe side." She would only take one—"Where d'you think I'm going, Timbuctoo?"

He went with her, unhappy about her going, to the front door. He didn't want to be left alone in this time and place where he didn't belong.

"You will come back?" he asked anxiously.

"Of course I will." She patted his cheek again. For a moment, he fancied she had been about to kiss him. He wished she had. He wished he was grown-up enough to kiss her.

"I'll be as quick as I can," she promised. "And while I'm away I should lock this door and not let anyone in, you know?—unless it's someone you're sure of, like Pete. He's all right. You can trust him, Howie."

From his bedroom window he watched her cross the court-yard towards the archway. First Pete had suddenly found urgent work that must be done, and now Tina, out of the blue, had just as suddenly come up with the excuse of having to go home to titivate herself up. Almost as if they had deliberately conspired together to leave him alone in the flat. But it couldn't be like that. If he couldn't trust Tina, he couldn't trust anyone.

He limped back to the settee to seat himself and swing his legs up from the floor. Twenty to four. He had been here in 1974 for something over twenty-four hours now. Which wasn't all that long, but still long enough, one would have thought, in which to have put together a reasonable picture of the past five years. But as it was, that picture was still a damn'

135

sight more holes than pieces. It might help make it clearer if he were to put together what little he had been able to find, even though it would mean a deal of guesswork.

Like he would have to start off with a guess, but a fairly safe one, that the decision he had finally come to that afternoon back at school was to go straight into the firm. Knowing the way Dad felt about him going to Oxford, it was another fairly safe guess he had taken it badly. But badly enough for it to rankle through the next three years and finally blow up in that confrontation in front of the whole staff? Howell didn't think so. But that incident had taken place; he felt sure that the dream had been of something that had actually happened. Dad had turfed him out not because of a three-year-old disagreement, but because of something else. Almost certainly—another inspired guess—the same something that had turned Andy and Aunt Meg and Uncle Wilf and the rest of them against him.

And had Dad turfed him out of home as well as out of the firm? Could be. Or he could have walked out under his own steam. To come here to share this flat with Mick Debroy. Which was a natural enough thing to do—muck in with an old school friend instead of having the trouble of finding digs for himself. What wasn't natural at all was his getting himself a job with Solmex instead of with any one of a score of similar concerns who were not out-and-out rivals of the old man, any of which would have been happy enough to find a berth for him.

But no, Solmex it was. And then another gap, this time of two years, ending up in Mick's murder. And all he knew about that two-year span was that towards the end, if Pete was to be believed, he had been suffering from some kind of nervous strain. And that was it, the sum total of what he had been able to find out. Certainly not enough for him to be able to say whether he had made the wrong decision that fateful afternoon, that if he had gone to Oxford instead, both Dad and Mick would still be alive.

That he was still here in this time was proof itself that he hadn't learnt enough about those five years. But with Pete saying he had told him everything he knew, with Dad and

136

Mick dead, with Andy turned against him, and the rest, there was nobody else he could talk to, nobody else he could go to for help.

But there was. Howell swung his feet to the ground and sat up straight. There was someone who surely wouldn't have turned against him no matter what he had done. The only reason he had forgotten about her till now, he excused himself to himself, was obviously because subconsciously he had written her off as being too far away to be of any help. As if Switzerland was on another planet and the telephone hadn't been invented.

Aunt Meg and Uncle Wilf would certainly know where she could be reached by phone. He would simply tell them he had lost the number. They wouldn't refuse to tell him where his own mother could be reached. Then a trunk call—no matter if it cost the earth—and to save time he would just say he had a touch of amnesia and he'd turned to her as being the best one to help him fill the gaps in his memory.

She'd help—no doubt about that. And she'd worry like stink. Probably come belting back home to find out what it was all about. Which could mean complications, because with luck by then he would be back home in 1969 again, and the Howell of now back in possession. No—he kept forgetting—it would be all right, because the Howell of now would know all about it and be ready to cope.

He must get out of the way of thinking of himself and the other Howell as being two different people. They weren't, they were the same. Anything he started now he should be able to cope with easily enough when he caught up with himself in five years' time. But that only applied if the future was unalterable. Which it couldn't be, else why had he been brought here? It was all part of a circle of thought that led nowhere.

Coming to his feet, Howell limped into the hall. No need to leave the front door open, Tina wouldn't be back for ages yet. Apart from his car the courtyard was empty. A quiet lot, the neighbours. Pete and his woman, and the lady with the poodle were the only ones he'd seen.

Pete opened the door. Judging by appearances, he had been

137

telling the truth about having work to do. He had a stained rag in one hand, a long paint brush in the other, another brush between his teeth. He was, it seemed, accustomed to speaking through clenched teeth and brush.

"Ah, our man of mystery. Thought of something else I might be able to help with?"

"I wondered if I might use your phone?" Howell asked.

Pete removed the brush from his mouth with a flourish, stepped aside with another flourish. "Be my guest." He grinned. "This time you'll know where it is." And: "Nessa's out shopping."

On a Sunday afternoon? Howell let it pass; some shops did open on a Sunday. In the pigsty lounge a drawing board was propped up on a table. Pinned on it was a partly finished drawing in black and glaring red, a poster, by the look of it, advertising a sale of electrical goods.

He found his way to the rickety three-legged table, picked up the phone and dialled the operator. "I would like a number on the Ascot exchange, please. Gretton fourteen."

A bored female voice said: "I'll look up the number for you. Hold the line."

Perplexed, Howell met Pete's gaze.

"I don't get it," he said. "I give her the right number, and she tells me to hold on while she looks it up."

"The sort of number you gave went out with the ark. Nearly everywhere's automatic now." Pete came to his side and held out his hand. "Let me." He took the receiver from Howell's fingers.

"Yes?"—into the phone. And: "Thanks, love." He replaced the receiver, picked it up again, started to dial and then broke off in the middle to look up, marvelling: "That had you really thrown. You just didn't know what it was about. And you work in an office. Like you once said, you spend most of your time with the phone glued to your ear. If what you've got is just ordinary lost memory, you'd think a thing like knowing how to use a phone properly would stick, like being able to read or ride a bike. That number you were after—"

138

"My home," Howell said. "At least, what used to be my home."

"I was watching your face. You weren't acting—no one's that clever. You just didn't have a clue. It's more than just amnesia you've got. So I'm mad. So I've not mentioned it before, but I've had something to do with ordinary amnesia. A friend of mine, a boxer, got it. You've got something different. But it can't be like you say it is. Or can it? What I'm seeing now is the same Howell I've always seen, but with someone different inside, him as he was five years ago. Man—"

"I've given up trying to make people believe me," Howell said.

"Maybe it would help them believe if you could give them some idea how it was done. But seemingly you can't. At least it's a point in your favour you haven't tried to invent an explanation."

"I've thought about it a lot," Howell said. "I've heard of the power the mind can have over matter, but I don't know anything about it, how it's supposed to work. Perhaps, if you want something badly enough, if you think about it hard enough, you can make it happen. I don't know."

"Like making a hundred-to-one outsider win the Derby." Pete grinned sideways. "Sounds like there could be a fortune in it. And you wanted to find out what nineteen seventy-four was like?"

"Not that year in particular. I had to make up my mind about something. I worried about it for ages. I wished I could get a look at the future to see how things had worked out. I was actually wishing that when it happened. I don't know yet why I've been brought to this time in particular, unless it's because this is the end of the outcome of whatever decision I came to."

"The end of the outcome?" Pete's face cleared. "Oh, I see what you mean. Like the curtain's just come down on what it was you started five years ago. Can something come to an end like that? Never mind—" He started to dial again, listened— "It's ringing"—and handed the receiver to Howell.

Aunt Meg's voice sounded more vague and fluttery than ever. "Hello? Who is that?"

"This is Howell. I'm sorry to—"

"Howell?"—in a tone of disbelief. And then, with something approaching anger: "Howell, now, you know it's no use—"

"Don't ring off," he broke in quickly, for by her tone she had been about to do just that. "Please listen. It's very important I speak to Mother, but I've mislaid the number where she can be reached." He left it at that.

"Mislaid it?" Now she sounded perplexed. "You can't have lost it when you never had it. Only Wilfred and I know where Mildred's living now, and she made us promise not to tell you. You know very well how she feels about you after everything that happened. You know she wants to have nothing more to do with you."

So that was how it was. Howell was shocked, but not nearly as badly as he had thought he might be. For all his hope that Mother would be different from the rest, at the back of his mind the possibility must always have existed that what he had done had been too much even for her to take.

He would have to tell Aunt Meg the truth. Somehow—and God knows how he could get through to her—he had to make her understand that the Howell who was talking to her now wasn't the same Howell Mother didn't want to speak to any more.

Before he could start, the querulous, wavering voice came on the line again, complaining: "I don't think it's nice of you trying to trick me that way—"

Hopeless to try to make her understand. "Let me speak to Uncle Wilf," he begged.

"He's not here. He's at the office working on an urgent order, and he won't be back till very late. And it's no use you calling again, because he simply won't speak to you—you know that. And now I'm going to ring off."

She rang off.

"Another blank?" Pete asked with what seemed genuine sympathy.

Replacing the receiver, Howell nodded.

140

"My last hope," he said bleakly, suddenly realising what losing that last hope really meant—that his learning of all the events of the past five years was a key, the only key that could open the door back to his own time. Without it he was trapped here in this alien time where almost everyone, even his own mother, had turned against him, where he was suspected of having killed one of his friends, where somebody had tried to kill him, would almost certainly try again. He was trapped in an existence from which there was now no escape and, because of that, had now become a nightmare.

"You look like you could use a drink," Pete said after a while. Howell shook his head. "No."

"Only cooking sherry, anyway. Things can't be as bad as all that. You'll think of something." Pete looked down at his part-finished poster.

"Yes." Howell took a deep breath. "I'd better get back. Thanks for letting me use the phone." He reached for his wallet. "I don't know how much—"

Pete dipped one of his brushes in a can of black paint. "I'll let you know when the bill comes in." He peered over the top of the drawing board, one thick black eyebrow cocked. "That's if you're still here. Otherwise I'll have to dun the other you for it, won't I?"

Howell tried to smile at what had obviously been intended as a joke. "I'll leave a note for him," he said. "Just in case he's forgotten about it by the time I've caught up with him." At the door he added: "That's if ever I get back to my own time to start on the catching-up process."

He went back to his own flat. Closing the front door, he saw the envelope on the floor, obviously pushed under the door while he had been away. He stooped to pick it up. Just his name on it, no address. Probably Wharton having another shot at getting in touch. He ripped the envelope open, took out the folded sheet. Typed, it started without preamble.

I got to thinking after your friend rang earlier.

So no need to turn it over to read the signature. It was from

Andy. Which meant that Pete had tried to talk to him as he had said he had. Howell started reading again.

I got to thinking after your friend rang earlier. He called himself that—your friend—and for some reason that made me feel ashamed. I told myself that he couldn't know the whole story, but then it's always possible I don't either. To me, everything that happened is capable of only one explanation, and nothing you might say can alter the facts. But I feel now that I owe it to you to at least listen to whatever it is you want to say to me.

We could talk over your friend's phone, but I just can't take the risk of being overheard. If it got about I'd talked with you I'd almost certainly lose my job. You know how Mr. Sinclair feels about you. We'll have to meet somewhere, a place where there's no chance at all of our being seen together. I can't get away to come up to London, so you'll have to come down to Gretton. The only place I can think of where we might meet without any chance of being seen is the old farm, Pritchard's Farm, you must know it.

Howell knew it all right. He had played as a child in the buildings, and the place had been almost a ruin in those days. It was the so-called home farm of the Ferncroft Hall estate, and was about quarter of a mile behind the Hall itself. That the house itself, and the outbuildings, hadn't long ago been snapped up by one of those city types who went in for the profitable business of converting derelict country buildings into desirable country residences was because the farm was Company property on Company land and would one day be demolished to make way for Company development.

He resumed reading.

Although it's Sunday I'll be working most of the day in-voicing a rush order—so at least Aunt Meg hadn't lied about that—but I will be able to get away round about half past six. One of our vans is moving off shortly, and the driver has agreed to make a short detour to deliver this to you. He's not one of our men, so he doesn't know your name. He should be in London before five, so that should give you plenty of time to be here by six-thirty.

142

For God's sake don't let anyone see you in Gretton in case they find out it's me you've come to see. Don't tell anyone where you're going, and you must destroy this note as soon as you've read it. It's taken me five years of hard work to get where I am today. I don't want to lose everything for the sake of someone who has caused so much trouble.

It was signed *Andrew*—not "Andy"—*Brett*.

And it screamed to high heaven that it was a trap. Or rather the bait for a trap. A secret rendezvous in a derelict farm . . . Like something out of a fourth-rate murder mystery. And "murder" was certainly the operative word. One attempt had failed; this was another.

But all so blatant, so very obvious. And with a certain difference of approach. Last time the bait had been: "I can help you find out what you're trying to find out." Now it was: "I'll listen to what it is you want to say."

Howell read it through again. It was the style of writing he would have associated with an Andy five years older than the last time he had seen a specimen of his letter writing. The signature at the foot looked to be genuine enough. And if he were in Andy's place, all the precautions asked for were the same precautions he himself would have wanted before sticking his own neck out.

It was either the bait for another attempt to kill him, or else an offer that was another chance—and this time certainly the last chance—of finding out about the last five years, of finding the key back to his own time.

He couldn't afford to let that chance slip by. He had no choice but to accept the letter as genuine. And having done that, obey all its instructions.

11

IT WAS ALMOST QUARTER TO FIVE. Howell hadn't real-ised it was that late. Last time it had taken him over two hours to make the trip to Gretton, but then he hadn't been sure of the earlier part of the route, and this time he was, and he had become more accustomed to the car, more confident of himself as a driver. But even so, it would take a bit of doing to get there for Andy's half past six. He took time out to scrawl a hurried note for Tina: *Back about nineish. Tell you about it then. No time to explain now. Howell.* He propped it against a cup on the kitchen table where she couldn't help but see it, and then, leaving, put the catch down on the front door lock so that all she would have to do was push or even only knock and it would open.

As usual the courtyard was deserted. In his car he checked the petrol. The something over two gallons in the tank would be more than enough to get him there. He could fill up again on the way back. That's if he would be the one making that journey. With luck, that would be a job for the other Howell. And the explaining to Tina. And then something that hadn't really occurred to him before. If Andy's letter was genuine, and if things worked out as he hoped, it would mean it would be five years before he saw Tina again. Five years . . . He would find himself back at school in 1969, knowing that the next time they met would be at a party on a Friday evening in 1974. So why hadn't he gone to see her before then? Why, knowing now how he felt about her, had he kept away from her all that time, not seeing her till that stupid office party? And then to meet as strangers . . . It didn't make sense. Unless it was that something would happen to him on the journey back home to his own time, so that he would arrive back in 1969 with his memory wiped clean of everything that had taken place here in 1974. But if that was the case, what was the point of being brought here to find out what the future was like if he wasn't going to be allowed to remember anything about it? None of it made sense. Thinking about it, trying to reason it out, was just waste of time. He reached for the starter.

There was little traffic on the Sunday afternoon streets. This time it took only forty minutes to reach Surbiton. Another half hour, almost six o'clock now, and he was in the friendly-familiar outskirts of Epsom—sun-warm russet walls, square red-and-white towers topped with glistening weathervanes, fold upon fold of distant, gently rolling green hills.

Ten minutes later and he was prepared for the first sight of the square Norman tower of Gretton church, showing above the tree tops. With the village itself still some distance away, he chose a place where the road widened to brake, pull onto the grass verge and draw up alongside a gap in the hedge.

From here, away across the fields, he could see the two long roofs of the main factory building, could make out the thatched tops of some of the older village cottages. And from here, having regard for Andy's fears, obeying all his instructions—except one: the letter wasn't destroyed but tucked inside his wallet—it would be safest to go the rest of the way on foot. He spent a few moments visualising the factory and its surrounds, wondering which would be the safest way of reaching the farm without being seen.

It would have to be the longest way round, he decided. Come upon the place from behind. It would take some time, might make him late for Andy's six-thirty, but it would be the safest . . .

From all points of view, for it would also mean he would be

approaching the place from the most unlikely quarter, from the very last direction anyone waiting there would expect him to come from. If the letter was bait, if the farm had been made into a trap, he had no intention of walking into it blindly.

He started walking along the quiet, dusty road. A stile reminded him of a forgotten short-cut, a path across the field that saved at least a few minutes and brought him out at the top of Gretton Lane with the factory lay-out over on the left. He continued ahead, the buildings—looking out of place in their rural setting—he had never noticed that before—falling behind. Twenty past six, his watch told him, and he quickened his pace.

The awaited turning on the left—he couldn't remember how long it was since the last time he had been this way—was a narrow winding lane with a near-lunar surface and uncared-for hedges that reached tall and ragged into the clear blue sky. And so dense that he was unable to see anything of what lay behind them, that it was like walking along the bottom of a green gorge.

Had the farm a rear entrance that would mean a break in the hedge on the left? He couldn't remember. Common sense said there was bound to have been one at some time or other. The farmhouse itself fronted on the road that dead-ended at the farm and was actually a continuation of the wide drive that linked the Hall, now the Company offices, with Gretton Lane. Behind the farmhouse, forming with it a hollow rectangle, were the more or less empty shells of what had once been stables and cow sheds. As he recalled, another derelict building stood a little distance away, probably the remains of a barn. And again as memory served him—it was a lifetime since he had played his own private game of cops and robbers or whatever there—the approach to the buildings, from this side, was over open, exposed ground. Which wasn't so good.

If this was a trap—his pulse quickened; he was aware of cold patches under his armpits—and the same pattern as before was going to be followed, then whatever was intended to happen to him would be arranged to look like an accident. But not a car this time, surely. Nobody would be careless enough to get themselves knocked down and killed by a car in an otherwise deserted farmyard. It would be something else—falling masonry, a collapsing floor, something like that. At least shooting was out, which was something to be thankful for.

The break in the hedge was so narrow, so overgrown, that Howell almost missed it, even though he had been watching out for it. Not a gate, as he had fancied it would be, but a stile. Or rather the rotting remains of an old wooden stile. And beyond it, no trace left at all now of the path that must once have cut through the field of long grass to the cluster of buildings not much more than a stone's throw away.

Standing well out of sight behind the hedge, peering cautiously through the branches, he inspected a scene that was much as he remembered it, buildings looking to be no more tumble-down now than the last time he had seen them. A peaceful, innocent scene in which nothing moved, in which nothing looked to be wrong or out of place. Just the crumbling red-brick ruins of a farm, lazing snugly in the early evening sunshine. And then, for all the warmth of that sunshine, Howell shuddered, suddenly afraid, so afraid that it was an effort to hold on to himself, to prevent himself turning and running back down the lane to climb into his car and drive as far away from here as he could.

The spasm passed. He drew a deep breath, trying to steady himself. No matter how afraid he felt, no matter what might be lying in wait for him ahead, he had to go on. Even if there was only one chance in a million of the letter being genuine and Andy waiting for him in one of those buildings, he still had to go on. It was either that or resigning himself finally to being marooned in this nightmare time where everything was wrong.

He let his gaze travel slowly along the line of buildings. If the letter was genuine—he glanced at his watch; twenty to seven; he was already late—then the most likely place for Andy to be waiting in now was the house itself, the least ruined building of the four. And by the same token, if this was a trap, that again was the most likely place. Or was that too obvious?

It would be safest to assume that somebody was there now,

waiting and watching, keeping an eye on both front and rear approaches. His first move would be to get close to the house without that somebody seeing him. There was a way in which that might be accomplished, by taking advantage first of the cover of the ditch that must lie on the other side of the hedge—he hoped it would be dry, that there hadn't been any rain for the last few weeks—then the cover of the tall windowless wall of the barn. All it needed was some way of negotiating the stile without exposing himself during the process. He managed it by crouching and wriggling through underneath. To drop then into the ditch, not dry, but at least no water, only a thin layer of glutinous mud that sucked at his hands and knees as he crawled along. After what he thought must be about a score of yards he carefully raised his head to peer through the long-stemmed grass to find he had estimated correctly, that from this point the towering back of the roofless barn completely masked the other buildings. He climbed out of the ditch to run, crouching, to the wall, there to lean against it while he regained his breath, lost after even such small exertion.

So far so good. He waited a few minutes for his heart to stop thumping against his chest. His ankle started to ache and he stooped to feel the bruise, finding that Tina's makeshift bandage had come unstuck and was hanging down. Taking the handkerchief away he put it in his pocket. A dog barked somewhere, the sound probably coming from one of the houses of Gretton Lane, not all that far away. Invisible from where he stood, he could see the silvery tops of the two main factory buildings and, a short distance to the right, the small complexity of grey slate slopes of the roof of the Hall.

His breath back, his heart normal again, he edged along the wall to the corner, dropping then to his hands and knees before peering round. And from here the farmhouse itself was still hidden, as he had hoped it might be, but only just, by the corner of the brick shell of the old stables. Head down, shoulders hunched, he crossed the few feet of open space to the rear stable wall. Now he was able to see into the barn, empty but for piles of broken bricks, some rotting timbers and rusty sheets of corrugated iron, and a tangle of metal from which protruded a broken wheel and a rump-shaped seat, all that was left of some piece of field equipment.

To get to the other end of the stables he had to force a way, hands well above his shoulders, through a dense mass of nettles. He peered round another corner. And now he was almost at the house, its end wall and two gaping, glassless windows only a few yards away. Empty windows; he could be sure of that because the sunlight was full on them. He ran to the wall between them so that, his back against the warm bricks, he could look first into one, then the other, making sure the rooms inside were indeed both empty.

And now he was here—an echo of the past when he had played cops and robbers with himself here, as he was doing now—with his memory sharpened by the views through the windows, he was all the better able to recall the general lay-out of the place. A very large hall dominated the house, stone-flagged, low-beamed, with four doors—or was it six?—leading from it, and a central staircase that went up to a balcony that was really only an open passage; and a flight of stone steps—it was all coming back—leading from a trap-door in the cubby-hole under the staircase down to the cellar. Eight rooms at least downstairs, and the same number upstairs. All shapes and sizes with any number of crooks and crannies and unsuspected corners. A schoolboy's paradise. And if he had to lie in wait for someone, which room would he choose?

Upstairs, he fancied, because from there you'd see more, even if it would mean dashing back and to between the front windows and the back. But there was a little room right at the top of the staircase from which, if you left the door open, you would be able to look out of a window at the back of the house and at the same time watch the hall and the front door, all without moving from the one spot. And that was the room he would choose.

And how well, he wondered, did his invisible enemy know the place? Well enough, evidently, to have chosen it as the site of a trap. But not, Howell was willing to bet, as well as a certain schoolboy had come to know it through innumerable sessions of cops and robbers. Advantage victim. And if the enemy thought that his intended victim would be entering by the orthodox method of a door, then he was sadly mistaken. Advantage number two to victim. Or was this all unnecessary after all? Had the letter really come from Andy, and was the sender in the house now, perhaps in the hall, sitting at the bottom of the stairs waiting for him to show up so that they could have their little chat? There was only one way to find out.

He rubbed the palms of his hands down the sides of his trousers, assessing the size of the nearest window. As a boy he had clambered through that very one by the simple expedient of grasping the ledge to haul himself ignominiously head-first into the room. Now, taller, he was able to reach up to grip the top of the window frame and swing his legs up and over the ledge without touching it. He landed lightly enough for one who had never performed that gymnastic before, only making a soft scuffling as his feet slithered over the dust and rubble on the floor. Only a faint sound, one that couldn't have carried any distance. But Howell stayed where he was for a minute or two, frozen in the position in which he had landed, holding his breath while he listened. And it seemed to him that, straining, he caught a whisper of sound that was an echo of his own scuffling.

Almost certainly imagination, he assured himself. But stupid to write it off just like that. Far better to regard it as a positive sound and behave accordingly. If he had to guess at its direction, he would have said from upstairs, from one of the bedrooms over his head, perhaps from the best-bet room at the top of the stairs. It would be best to assume that the enemy was as familiar with the house as he was himself.

Either falling stonework or collapsing floor—he still thought it would be either one of those. And upstairs would be where accidents of that nature would be most likely to happen. The floors down here were stone flagged, the ceilings—of this room anyway—looking to be fairly sound. Upstairs the floors would be rotting boards and the ceilings death traps of rain-rotted plaster and beams.

It might even be a booby-trap. That was something that hadn't occurred to him before. Something rigged up, say, to collapse with the opening of a door; he could think of a dozen ways, with the originator far away establishing an alibi just to be on the safe side. A distinct possibility, that, and so it would be just as well if he provided himself with a stick, something with which to push open doors without stepping over the threshold.

There was nothing in this room that would serve. Howell tip-toed silently to the door that led to the hall. Hanging from one hinge, he had to lift it before it would move, scraping over the floor as it opened safely inwards. He dropped to his knees before peering into the hall, not nearly so large as his memory had told him, shrunken, as most places tend to become, after the absence of years.

The front door, a massive affair, was closed. And had been that way for quite a while, if the thick layer of brick and mortar rubble on the floor behind it was anything to go by. The staircase, that too not as impressive as he had thought it to be, looked to be safe enough, even though one bannister rail had come away completely, and the other was sagging dangerously to one side. Some of the rails still clung to the bannister, but most of them had worked loose and fallen to the floor. Solid-looking lengths of wood, just the sort of thing he had in mind to serve the dual purpose of booby-trap-springer and weapon.

He started to move towards them, then stopped, looking down at the floor that was littered with the gritty debris of decay, the stone flags where he was standing covered with the off-white snow of plaster that had flaked and powdered from the ceiling. And in that snow—his pulse faltered then raced—footprints. He bent over them—fresh footprints, no doubt about their newness—and proof positive that someone was either here with him in the house now, or else had been and gone again not so very long ago. Only one track, coming from the rear of the house, leading towards the cubby-hole affair under the staircase.

The cellar? Was that it? Fatal accident caused by falling down a flight of stone steps onto a stone floor. And how did they propose getting him to stand at the top of those steps while they did the pushing? By getting him to follow these footprints. *Look, see how I've left a trail behind me without realising it. Be clever and follow and sneak up behind me.*

Which he might have done, Howell thought, and fallen for it, if the trail didn't look so obvious, each footprint clearly defined. Whoever had made them would be in the room under the stairs now, standing to one side of the sloping doorway, waiting for the victim to follow and enter. To be sent flying head-first down on to the stone floor of the cellar.

Silently, still stooping, he reached to pick up one of the rails. Heavy, nicely balanced, with even a carved base to serve as a grip, it made a very handy weapon. Straightening, he started to move again, not following the tracks towards the rear of the staircase, but in the opposite direction, away from it, round the front of the stairs and down the other side so that now he was approaching the cubby-hole and whoever was waiting there from behind. He wondered, back pressed against the panelling, if that someone knew there were two entrances to the room, one on either side of the staircase. No need to wonder; the door on this side was no longer there. Cudgel held ready, heart pounding, Howell went round the corner and into the room in one swift silent move.

It was empty. Nobody was waiting behind the opposite doorway. He had guessed wrongly about that part, but seemingly not about the cellar being used for a fatal accident. The trapdoor was open, had only recently been opened, for there was no grit or rubble in the rim where it rested when closed. If the footprints weren't part of a trap, why then had the entrance to the cellar been opened up? Surely the enemy couldn't be down there? Come into my parlour . . . They couldn't expect him to be that naïve.

Nerves tense and tingling, the cudgel held ready, he moved forward one silent, cautious step at a time until he was standing on the edge of the opening, able to look down into the cellar, the flight of worn stone steps leading down into semi-darkness. He had never been down there. As a boy he had always been afraid that the trap-door might fall behind him and he not strong enough to push it open again. He didn't know how far the cellar extended, if there were more than one, if—

The blow caught him in the small of his back, hurling him forwards, face-first, into the opening. It was the cudgel, held firmly at shoulder level, that saved him from serious injury, perhaps worse—breaking the impact of his fall by catching against the side of the opening and becoming jammed there, in the gap where a brick had crumbled away, long enough to cause him to swing sideways then backwards, so but instead of hurtling down head-first he struck the steps first with his hip, then his shoulder, to go sliding down on his back, bumping from step to step, stunned rather than injured by that first impact, unconscious even before he reached the ground.

12

HE KNEW HE HAD BEEN UNCONSCIOUS, he didn't know for how long. His watch was still going, he could hear it when he put it to his ear, but it was too dark to see it. Not completely dark, not pitch black, for there was light of a kind, a pearly greyness filtering in through a gap on one side of the closed trap-door.

He didn't think he could have been out for very long, for there had been no period of half-and-half wooziness; right from the first moment of returned consciousness he had been fully aware of where he was and what had happened.

Howell stared bleakly into the darkness. He had thought he was being so clever, so damn' clever . . . Figuring out what the enemy was up to, anticipating his moves, figuring how to turn the tables. And he'd finished up a mug, standing right on the edge of the cellar, right on the spot marked for him. Or maybe the enemy, waiting his chance, had just taken advantage of the opportunity when it was offered. Not that that mattered a damn right now.

A question of getting organised. First, find out if he was still all in one piece. He was sore and aching in a score of places, but he didn't think there were any bones broken. His arms were all right. He used them to push himself up from the floor. His legs were all in order. He knelt on them, then came to his feet. And had to lean against the wall to stop from falling down again. The worst places were his left shoulder and hip. But once the floor had settled down he should be able to walk.

Give it a few minutes, and spend that time getting himself sorted out. The enemy was out to kill him, the car attempt was proof of that. So how come, after he had been at the mercy of that enemy—and it had to be the same—he was still alive? But it was possible that was intended to be merely a temporary state of affairs. Perhaps the coup de grace was to come later. But not all that much later. The someone who had set the trap couldn't be sure that his victim had obeyed the letter's instructions and not told anyone where he was going. Which meant he just couldn't secure the trapdoor on his unconscious victim and then go away, leaving him to die of starvation or something. He had to get him away from the farm, alive or dead, before anyone came looking for him. Which meant the enemy might return at any time. Which further meant—Howell looked up at the grey light—the sooner he got the hell out of here, the better.

He tried standing unaided again. The floor swayed and steadied. Feeling for the bottom step, his foot dislodged something loose. His makeshift weapon, he discovered by the feel, and pushed it to one side. Steadying himself with one hand against the wall, he started to climb. Four steps, and his head touched the trap-door. He climbed to the next one before testing it with his hands, finding it immovable, as he had expected, but not, he fancied, bolted or screwed down, for it seemed to move a fraction at one side, as if it were being held down by something heavy on top. Another two steps and now he was able to get his back and shoulders to the job. The door creaked, lifted another fraction, and then refused to move further. Bolted after all. And half a dozen men all pushing upwards at the same time would never force off a bolt from below. It needed a lever. A lever . . .

He backed down the steps, stopped at the foot, felt round for the cudgel. Mahogany, he hoped. Or oak, good hard oak. Please, God, make it a harder wood than that holding the screws of the bolt.

There was a place into which the lever could be inserted, the same brick gap that had come to his aid once before. It took the end of the rail as if it had been carved out expressly for that purpose, but only a few inches. Please, God, make that enough. Gripping the other end with both hands he steadily exerted pressure, very steadily, almost afraid to breathe, afraid of the crack that would tell him—

Wood splintered, and his heart stood still. But the lever was still intact. Relief was a flood of ice-cold water. Now he was able to push the rail further into the gap. A far better leverage now. He tensed himself, feet apart, one shoulder set against the wall, teeth gritted. Wood splintered again, and then metal screeched against metal. A miniature avalanche of rubble and brick dust came cascading down as the door gave so suddenly Howell nearly fell backwards down the stairs. He used the end of his piece of wood to finish off the job, pushing the door up until it fell back with a loud clatter in a cloud of rising dust.

He climbed up into the room under the staircase, and then reaction set in so that he had to lean against the sloping doorway until he had stopped shaking. Quarter past eight, his watch told him when his hands were steady again; he must have been unconscious longer than he had thought.

And now out of the house as quickly as possible, before the enemy returned. He left the same way he had come in, this time climbing through the window instead of swinging bravado through it. Now he was able to breathe freely again, now he felt safe. And for all the aches and pains of his bruises, filled with an odd sense of elation. He let it have its way with him.

His original intention had been to get back to his car in double-quick time, climb into it and drive back to London. And he would be back where he had started, still marooned in this alien time. He had taken the risk of coming here in the hope, faint as it had been, of having a chance to talk to Andy. He had risked his life then; why not try the direct approach again, when this time all he would be risking was another rebuff? And in his present condition—filthy, dried blood on his hands, clothes torn and streaked with mud from the ditch and filth from the cellar, and with the letter to back up his story—there was a good chance that Andy might be shocked into giving him a hearing. Any other normal curious person would, anyway. The letter . . . He fumbled for it in his wallet, suddenly afraid he might have been searched while unconscious and the letter removed. But it was still there.

All set, then. He made his way along the side of the house towards the front, keeping well into the wall, pushing through bushes and briars. The road leading from the farm past the Hall to Gretton Lane was deserted. He walked along it, in the centre, almost jauntily, stopping after a while to look back at the ruined farm. What had happened back there had become oddly unreal, as if it had all been part of some game he had been playing, an extension of the cops and robbers of his schooldays.

But it had been for real, no game. But for the lucky break of having that bannister rail with him he would never have been able to get out of the cellar. He remembered the avalanche that had been dislodged by the trap-door being opened. There was no doubt that whoever had closed and bolted it on him had gone to the trouble of covering it with grit and rubble, perhaps a deep enough layer to disguise the very presence of the door. The slow death of starvation . . . That cellar had been intended as his grave. Shivering, Howell turned to resume walking.

Still broad daylight, there were still lights on in some of the Hall windows. Someone was always working there, weekdays, Sundays and holidays alike; there had always been urgent orders that had to be got away immediately, always vans leaving for London Airport.

Two men, both strangers to Howell, were talking earnestly by one of the several cars drawn up alongside the main entrance. They broke off to stare unabashed at him, looking him up and down. He ignored them, even smiling to himself. So he must look like a tramp or worse. So what the hell. At the gates, the porter was in his lodge, so he was spared a second staring match, not that, in his present mood, he cared one little jot. Gretton Lane was empty. The house where Andy lodged was only a few minutes away. Howell flung open the gate and rapped on the door with all the assurance of someone who knows he will be made welcome. And if the owner of the house—what was his damn' name?—tried turning him away, he'd just push him aside and barge in.

It was Andy himself who opened the door. Nondescript fair hair as unruly as ever; as ugly as ever too, with that too-broad nose of his, and that thick-lipped mouth. In blue shirt sleeves, tieless, and managing to look more like an overgrown schoolboy than the rising young executive he probably was.

A brief instant of polite puzzlement. Then his face changed. "You, again." He seemed on the point of slamming the door. Then he took in Howell's appearance, and his expression changed yet again. "What the devil have you been doing with yourself?"

An opening too good to be missed. Howell had the letter out ready. "Only what this told me to do."

"What's this?" Andy took it from him with some reluctance, frowned at it, started to read. And exclaimed aloud when he came to the signature at the foot. He looked up, indignant as well as perplexed. "I didn't write this!"

"I know that now," Howell replied drily. "I didn't think there was much chance it came from you when I first got it. But I went to the farm just the same. And nearly got myself killed for my trouble."

"Killed?" The other stared at him. "You mean you had an accident there?"

"I wouldn't call being pushed into a cellar and the trap-door bolted on top of me an accident. Neither would I call being lured to a narrow alley and almost run down by a car that came deliberately at me. That was this morning."

Andy couldn't take it in. "You're trying to say someone's deliberately trying to kill you?"

Howell contented himself with a nod. Better to underplay the thing than be all dramatic.

"That's impossible." Andy looked down at the letter. "But there's this, and it's not from me." He looked up again. "And something's happened to you right enough." He stepped aside.

"You'd better come in, Howell." And as Howell edged by into the narrow hall, "Trying to murder you? Do you know why?"

"If I knew that," Howell replied from the foot of the stairs, "I might have some idea who it is. But that isn't why I want to see you, why I tried to get to talk to you last night."

"And again this morning, over the blower. Getting quite persistent."

"Who did you tell about Pete ringing you up?" Howell asked.

"Pete being that friend of yours, I suppose. Who did I tell?" Andy turned from closing the front door. "And what do you want to know that for?"

"Because whoever wrote that letter knew about Pete ringing you up."

"I see. Clever." Andy rubbed the side of his nose. "But that won't help any. Who did I tell? Everyone I could ruddy well think of. I went out of my way to broadcast it. Just so's they'd all know it was you trying to get in touch with me, not the other way round, and I wanted no part of it. Hell—that part of the letter that says I've got my job to think of is true enough. If it got round I'd been cohorting with you, I wouldn't have a job. Not with Trowman."

"I seem to have made a very good job of turning everyone against me," Howell said.

At which the other was frankly astonished. "Christ, man, what did you expect after what you did?"

"That's just it," Howell said equably enough. "I don't know what I've done. I've got no idea at all. That's why I wanted to see you, to ask you to help fill in some of the gaps. You could say I've lost part of my memory."

It seemed the other was now past being surprised at anything. "Why only 'could say'?"

"Because that's the handiest way of describing what's happened to me. That's what everyone else puts it down to."

"You mean you've been ill? Or are you ill now?" And then, with some reluctance: "You'd better come upstairs and sit down. At least we've got the place to ourselves. The Humphreys won't be back till late."

He led the way upstairs to a landing and into quite a large

and well-furnished combined bed and sitting room. There was a desk, two easy chairs, a sideboard, even a settee. The bed itself was tucked away almost out of sight, flat against one rose-pink wall.

He nodded towards one of the chairs. "A drink, Scotch?" He poured it out without waiting for any reply, added soda from a globular syphon and ice from a Wedgwood thermos tub. "Here." He put the glass in Howell's hand, lifted his own glass without offering a greeting or toast. "So what's all this about lost memory?"

Howell sipped his drink. "Which would you rather have, the unbelievable truth or a believable lie?"

Andy lowered himself to the other easy chair. "Try me with the truth," he invited.

Howell did, telling it in as few words as possible, as dispassionately as possible. When he had done, the other rose to his feet, refilled his glass automatically at the sideboard array, remembered he had a guest, brought the bottle and the syphon over to top up Howell's glass, then replaced them carefully on the sideboard. All in silence. He didn't speak until he had sat down again and tried his fresh drink. Then:

"I believe you, Howell. Or rather I believe that you believe that what you've told me really happened the way you've said it did. It couldn't, of course—"

"Of course," Howell agreed laconically.

"I thought at first it was some sort of gag—"

"So did Pete. He thought I was out to get folk thinking there was something wrong with my mind, so that if the police ever did get round to arresting me for Mick's murder—" Howell broke off, shrugging. "Nuts—you know; bonkers, off my marbles, didn't know what I was doing. I'm told I'd been getting blackouts, anyway. Genuine ones, seemingly."

Andy studied the contents of his glass for a few moments. "A breakdown," he said. "That must be it. Some kind of nervous breakdown that made you lose your memory. I've heard of that before."

"Just for fun, another of my friends thinks I've been got at in some way, doped and hypnotised, she thinks; brainwashed into believing what I do believe. She's a grand girl, but she's been seeing too many films."

"But somebody killed Debroy, and someone's had two tries at killing you. Too much of a good thing." Andy came to his feet. "I'm going to call Mr. Sinclair."

Howell smiled drily over the rim of his glass. "I can't see you getting any change out of Uncle Wilf. Not according to Aunt Meg, anyhow."

"I'm going to try him. Help yourself to another drink if you feel like it." Andy eyed him up and down. "The bathroom's next door if you feel like getting rid of the top layer. A clothes-brush in that drawer." He took his glass with him downstairs.

Howell took off his jacket, shook it and laid it on the back of his chair. Rolling up his shirt sleeves, he went out on to the landing. The bathroom door was open. He ran hot water into the basin.

Ten minutes later, when he returned to the bedroom, Andy was holding his jacket at arm's length and brushing it.

Howell rolled his sleeves down. "That feels better." Some of his joints had stiffened up a little. "Better still when I've had a bath. Any joy with Uncle Wilf?"

"He'll be here as soon as he can." Andy draped the now reasonably clean jacket over the arm of the settee. "I caught him in the middle of dinner. I just told him you were here and that I thought he ought to hear what you had to say because it might mean things weren't quite like we thought they were. Something like that."

"I might not be responsible after all for what I'm supposed to have done?"

"You're responsible all right, there can't be much doubt about that, but there might be more to it than meets the eye."

"Mitigating circumstances." Howell smiled faintly. "Got a comb I can borrow? Thanks"—as Andy pointed to the corner dressing table. "And just what is it I've done that's got every-one's back up?"

"You want it just like that? It's quite something."

"So it seems."

The other seemed nettled by the almost sarcastic tone. "All

161

right. In a nutshell, you brought Trowman Chemicals to the verge of bankruptcy after causing them to lose millions of pounds, you lost some five hundred men their jobs, helped kill your father, murdered your best friend."

Comb in hand, Howell turned from the dressing table mirror. "Quite something. And there's no doubt I did all that?"

"There's no doubt. You don't seem all that surprised."

"I think I was expecting something worse. What, I don't know." Howell turned back to the mirror again. "I don't see how it could be any worse, though. I think maybe my not throwing a fit or something must be because I feel inside I'm not really to blame for any of those things. I don't see how I could be. Bankrupt the firm? Kill the old man? Oh no. I particularly don't like the notion of being held responsible for his death." His hair seemed fairly clear of the dust and grit of the farmhouse. Replacing the comb, he turned round again to lean against the dressing table, his hands, behind him, gripping its carved edge. "I think you'd better put me in the picture, Andy."

"I'll tell you all I know. Mr. Sinclair should be able to add to it. I'm just a staff employee; I only know what everyone else here knows, nothing of the personal side of it. Well, that afternoon at school, you decided to do as your mother wanted and go straight into the firm. Did you know that?"

Howell nodded. "I guessed."

"You spoke to your father about me, and he found me an opening. I'm grateful to you for that, Howell. And him, of course. I'm doing very well. This—" His gesture took in the room. "Convenient, handy for work. I'm thinking about getting married. Then I'll build my own house. But that's not what you want to hear. Your father wasn't too put out about you not going to Oxford. You told me afterwards you'd half an idea he knew how ill he was.

"He started you off right at the very bottom, in despatch, and he made you work your way up through every department, a few months in each, working night and day for damn all. You told me yourself you were only being paid two quid a week. They said—you know office gossip—he was deliberately working you to death to see if you could take it. And afterwards, they said that though you hadn't shown it, you must have resented it like hell all the time.

"You came into the firm the same day as me—Monday, the eighth of September, 'sixty-nine. Everyone was working flat out, getting ready to launch a new product. I remember it all right. Rhinex, it was called. A cold remedy. No better than a dozen others, and no worse. But with a new gimmick that was going to catch on. It was a capsule, and part of the formula was contained by the capsule, and the other part was embodied in the substance of the capsule itself. It should have been ready to market before the cold season started, but a snag in production held things up. It was finally scheduled to be launched at the beginning of March. We'd spent over quarter of a million on promotion. And a fortnight before the day set for launching it, Solmex came out with Rhynex. Identical product, identical formula, almost identical packaging. You can forget about coincidence—"

"Somebody sold us out," Howell said.

"And how. We worked it out that for them to have launched it when they did meant they must have had all the information about it no later than September of the previous year."

"I begin to see," Howell said slowly. "I came in September, the sell-out was in September. Another coincidence they couldn't accept."

"A quarter of a million," Andy said. "That's what we dropped on it. We put Rhinex out, and it flopped like a wet haddock. And that was only the start. There was a new vitamin tablet, a tranquilliser, a dyspepsia mixture. Every one pipped at the post by Solmex. God knows how much went down the drain. We closed part of the Birmingham plant, laid off some of the staff here. I was lucky to be kept on. And then word got round that you and your father were at loggerheads, that he was openly accusing you of being the traitor. A lot more thought the same way, but if you were being paid for it, and why else would you do it—except maybe revenge—then what were you doing with the money? You still didn't have two pennies to rub together.

You were too clever to throw it around, they started saying; you were tucking it away somewhere.

"And then—let's see—the July of 'seventy-two, it would be—you and Mr. Trowman had a real set-to in the main office in front of everybody. It finished up with him telling you to get out. Which you did; you even left home. And you know something else?"

"The leakages stopped at the same time," Howell said.

"Just in time to save Trowman Chemicals from bankruptcy. It clinched the matter where you were concerned, of course. Nobody was all that surprised when we heard you'd actually gone to work for Solmex. And apart from all that, everyone felt certain your father would never have accused you openly the way he did on just gossip and coincidences. He must have known something.

"He never seemed to get over that last quarrel with you. He carried on working, but you could see he was under a strain. He died suddenly—"

Andy broke off to ask anxiously: "You did know he had died, Howie?"

It was good to have Andy call him "Howie" again. "I knew," Howell told him.

"Thank heaven for that. I came out with it without thinking. He died suddenly at his desk. Mrs. Trowman, your mother, left almost straight after the funeral. She sold out completely, lock, stock and barrel, everything. Like she didn't want to have anything left to remind her. She went to live in Geneva. Did you know the Sinclairs are living in your old home now, and that he's the Big White Chief?"

"I knew about my home. I guessed the other."

"Chairman of the board of directors." Andy smiled a little. "Talk about a fish out of water. They say Mrs. Trowman asked him to take over, and he had no choice. He's put on years these last two months. You wouldn't think he was the same person. Never smiles, goes round with a face like a thundercloud. He's going to crack up sooner or later, unless he can push the responsibility onto someone else. Which is why I felt certain he'd come running if he thought there was the slightest chance of you having been misjudged. He should be here by now."

Andy went over to the window to draw the curtain aside. "No sign yet."

"You haven't mentioned Mick Debroy," Howell said.

"Because I don't know anything about him." Andy let the curtain fall back. "Other than what I read in the papers. The police came down here. A Detective Inspector Mellor. Nice bloke. Wanted to know how you and Debroy got on together. All I was able to tell him was that you hit it off all right at school, but after that I couldn't say. I asked the inspector if he thought you'd really done Debroy in as most of the papers seemed to think. Not a very clever thing to ask a copper on a murder case, but he was the sort of bloke you could talk to. He said it wasn't such an open and shut case as the press seemed to be making out. For one thing, the police were sure that Debroy hadn't actually died in the garage where you found his body. He'd been done in some place else, and his body taken to the garage afterwards. He told me to keep that to myself for the time being. I thought it a bit odd, a detective like that trusting someone he didn't know with information that was obviously vital. But from what little I had to do with him I had him down as nobody's fool. The sort of bloke who has a reason for everything he does or says."

Howell leaned back in his chair and stared up at the ceiling.

"I don't know if I did sell the firm out," he said slowly. "I don't think I could have done. I can't imagine ever doing a thing like that, no matter how bad the provocation."

He brought his gaze down. "Do you think I did it, Andy?"

"Everything pointed to it being you."

"So it seems. But supposing it wasn't me, who else could it have been, Andy? Who else knew enough about—well, about that first product—Rhinex, was it called—to have been able to offer it to Solmex on a plate?"

The other smiled wryly. "If only you knew the hours we've spent talking about it over at the office. The thing is, any number of people had all the dope at their fingertips, and not all of them full-time company employees. Apart from the obvious ones—you and your father, Mr. Sinclair, the other directors—apart from those there were the chemists who'd worked on the formula, the sales promotion manager, the artist who designed the packing, the salesmen who would have to sell it—a list as long as your arm. We did tighten up security after that first leak, but it made no difference. The—"

It was the only just audible sound of a car drawing up outside that had made him break off. "That sounds like him." He drew the curtains aside again. "Yes, that's his Aston." At the door, he paused. "Look, Howie, I'll go down and talk to him first. Make it easier for you. Explain what's been happening to you."

"Suitably adjusted?" Howell wondered sardonically.

"No. I'll tell him exactly what you told me, and it's up to him to make what he pleases of it." Andy nodded towards the sideboard. "Pour yourself another drink."

There was a knock on the front door, and he went down to answer it, leaving the bedroom door open behind him. Perhaps an invitation to Howell to listen in if he felt that way inclined.

Howell didn't. But it was something, he felt, to have been afforded the chance. Proof of a kind that Andy was being above-board about everything.

He pushed himself up out of his chair—God, his side was sore and stiff—and limped to the sideboard to pour himself another glass of soda water. It would be some time before he got the acrid taste of the farmhouse dust and grit out of his mouth. He took the drink over to the window, there to peer down at Uncle Wilf's Aston Martin. The last time he had seen it, it had been stuck in the garage at home and he had thought it must be the old man's. But it wasn't his home any more, and the old man's driving days were over.

And so much for Andy's version of the last five years. But obviously not a complete record. That he was still here in 1974 could only mean there was still more he had to find out. He fancied he could hazard a guess as to what that might be.

Draining the glass, Howell set it down on the window ledge. Either he had killed Mick Debroy, or someone else had. That the police hadn't arrested him during the two months since the murder would suggest they had decided he must be innocent. Which meant the murderer was someone else. And it was a million pounds to a wooden penny that that someone wasn't going to do any talking about what he had done. Which meant again that there would always be one gap in those five years he would never be able to fill. Or could it possibly be that the reason he had been brought here was to solve the murder? Now, that was an idea . . .

"Howell?" Andy's voice came up from below, and he took this new idea with him out onto the landing and down the stairs.

To where Uncle Wilf stood waiting with his back against the front door. Three months, by Howell's own time, since he had last seen him—the occasion then a half-term break at school —Aunt Meg in fluttery regatta pink frills, Uncle Wilf in countryman deerstalker and breeches. Only three months ago, five years by everyone else's reckoning, and so he was ready for the changes those years must have brought in someone who wouldn't see sixty again.

And Uncle Wilf had certainly aged. His hair—grey now instead of the remembered dark brown—had thinned and, receding from his high forehead, had lengthened an already long and narrow face. Deep lines had been cut between his eyes, from the sides of his nose to his mouth, from the corners of that unhappy mouth to the jaw. His eyes were part of the greyness of his sunken features, an impression of that sad colour rather than the colour itself. He wore thick, greenish tweeds— he always had worn tweeds, summer and winter alike, as if hoping they might add bulk and authority to his person.

He nodded, not smiling. "You look little the worse for your experience, Howell." There was a kind of welcome in his voice.

"You should have seen him before we cleaned him up, sir," Andy offered.

"Yes." He had the letter in his hand. "This, the signature, Brett. Would you say it was a fair copy?"

Andy nodded. "I'd say it was a very good copy, Mr. Sinclair."

"So we can assume that whoever wrote it must have had one of your signatures alongside him to copy from." Uncle Wilf held the letter up. "Do you mind if I keep this for a time?"

Howell shook his head. "You're welcome to it."

"Brett has told me something of what has been happening." Uncle Wilf slipped the letter in his pocket. "An incredible affair. Frankly—" He shook his head, clearly lost for something to say, not knowing what he was supposed to be expected to do about it. "And you say you haven't been to the police?"

Howell smiled a little. "Under the circs, just a waste of time, Uncle Wilf."

"Yes. Under the circumstances. Yes, I think I see what you mean. We must talk about it." He looked at his watch, patently unhappy about the whole situation. "I'm afraid I can't invite you home, Howell—"

Howell made it easy for him. "I know you can't. I never expected you to. If you're seen with me, you're likely to be outlawed too."

"Yes. But we must talk—"

"You're very welcome to the use of my room, Mr. Sinclair," Andy offered.

"Yes. Thank you, Brett, but I think—" Uncle Wilf looked at Howell. "I didn't see a car outside. Brett says you drove down from London."

"I left it in the road behind the farm."

"Behind— Denny Lane. I'll drive you there." And to Andy, a little stiffly: "Thank you for your trouble, Brett. We'll talk about it some other time. In the meantime it might be just as well if you didn't tell anyone that Mr. Trowman has been here."

"I won't, sir," Andy replied formally, and offered his hand, albeit with some hesitation, to Howell. "I hope things work out for you now, Howie. And watch your step."

"I will," Howell told him, and turned to follow Uncle Wilf out to the car.

The Aston Martin purred into life, whispered into motion.

"A long time since we've had anything to do with each other," the older man said awkwardly, gaze rigidly on the road ahead.

"So I've discovered," Howell replied easily.

168

"Yes. I keep forgetting. A strange situation, Howell. And when Margaret found you in my study—?"

"I thought Dad was still alive. I thought it was his office. I was after anything that would help me find out about myself."

"Yes. A strange situation indeed. Howell, I want to talk to you. Alone. That's why—here together like this. But I'm not sure I'd be doing right. May do more harm than good. A matter—" Uncle Wilf broke off to lapse into a silence that lasted until they were in the lonely lane behind the farm, drawing up behind Howell's car. Switching off the engine with an absent gesture he leaned back, still looking through the windscreen.

"Because of what's been happening to you, Howell, these attempts on your life, there's something you ought to know. But something for reasons of my own I never intended you should know. For old times' sake, if you want the reason. I owe your father a very great deal. I'm not going to get maudlin. But now your life's in danger, and that's an even better reason for telling you. Even though I may be doing you great harm in another way. Brett told me something about your blackouts. Have you been having treatment for them?"

"From a Dr. Wharton, so they tell me."

"Wharton. No, I don't know the name. A London man, obviously. A psychiatrist?"

"An ordinary G.P. so far as I know." Howell paused. "What's it all about, Uncle Wilf?"

"Yes." The other closed his eyes for a moment, opened them again, sighed. "Yes"—and turned to look at Howell for the first time. "It's something that happened a couple of months ago. Friday, the twenty-fourth of May—"

A date that rang a bell with Howell. "The day Mick Debroy was killed," he said.

"Yes." Uncle Wilf turned to stare ahead again. "The night Debroy was murdered. I worked late, I forget for what reason. It would be about six-thirty. Most of the staff had gone— I'm talking about the office here at the Hall. There was something I needed; a contract reference. Brett's department. I went to his office, but he had left. I looked through the papers on his desk, then I started to go through the desk drawers.

There was a letter. It was addressed to Brett, and it was from Martin Debroy. I knew the name, of course. I knew he was a Solmex man and that you and he were sharing a flat. The letter was ambiguously worded, but still made two things clear. That the two were in collusion, and that money had changed hands."

At which point Howell broke in, breathing incredulously: "Andy and Mick? You're saying Andy was the one selling the secrets and Mick was doing the buying? I don't believe it." And then remembered the brief case full of money, and was silent.

"I'm only telling you what happened," Uncle Wilf said. "I read the letter again. As proof that Brett was the traitor, it would never have stood up in a court of law. My chief consideration was to have you back in your rightful place at Trowman. But your name would have to be cleared first. And that could only be done by the guilty person being exposed. I couldn't take the risk of exposing Brett with only the letter to back up my accusations. I couldn't even risk firing him, in case he sued for wrongful dismissal. I needed more evidence. And it seemed to me there was a good chance that might be found at Debroy's home. Which you shared with him.

"I decided to get in touch with you. I didn't know where you were living, but I did know where you were working. In any case, I thought it might not be wise to go to your home in case Debroy were to see me and become suspicious. I rang your office on the off chance you might still be there. You weren't, a woman told me, you were out on a promotion job and wouldn't be back before nine, but you would be calling in at your office on your way back home.

"I left Gretton without telling anyone, not even Margaret, where I was going. I reached your office about half past eight and parked a distance away on the other side of the street in case anyone from your office were to see and recognise me. It was a wretched night, raining and windy. You arrived at about ten past nine and went into your office. I crossed over ready to buttonhole you when you came out again.

"You were only inside for a few minutes. When you came

out again I came from behind your car, where I'd been waiting. I don't think you knew me for a few moments. And I was shocked at the change in you. You looked as if you had been ill—pale, circles under your eyes. You stared right through me as if you were having trouble focussing. I forget what you did say when you did recognise me.

"My intention was to simply tell you about the letter and then suggest you went through Debroy's things at the flat you were sharing to see if there was anything incriminating amongst them. But I only managed to get as far as telling you about the letter and who it was from, and then your face changed—I don't think then you really knew what you were doing—you shouted something—I only managed to catch Debroy's name—and then you turned to make for your car.

"I tried to stop you. I was afraid of what you might do. The expression on your face . . . You pushed me aside, so roughly I tripped and fell in the gutter. By the time I'd picked myself up you were in your car and starting to move away. I ran across to where I'd left my car and started after you."

Uncle Wilf shook his head, gaze remote. "I can't remember much of that drive. I do remember asking myself what I'd do if I did manage to catch up with you, if I'd try to edge you off the road or if it would be best just to keep on your tail until you reached your flat—that had to be where you were going —and then try to stop you going inside. You were going after Debroy, that was obvious; I didn't even dare think what you intended doing to him.

"I lost you in the traffic—oh, two, three times—and managed to pick you up again. Then I lost you again when we were out in the suburbs and there wasn't all that much traffic. I turned into a long road, and there was no sign of you in either direction. I turned round and started back the way I had come. It was only by chance I caught sight of your car standing in a mews, through an archway. I stopped, climbed out of my car and ran through the arch just in time to see you climbing up what I first took to be a fire-escape, but turned out to be the stairs leading up to your flat. You had something in your hand, I couldn't make out what.

"I climbed the stairs behind you. The door at the top was closed. There were sounds coming from behind it, voices, shouting. The door wouldn't open. I was afraid to hammer on it, or shout, in case any of the neighbours heard and came to see what was happening. And then suddenly the noise stopped. The silence—the sudden silence—terrible. I was afraid, Howell. A coward. Afraid of what had happened inside the flat to cause that sudden silence, even more afraid of being involved.

"I backed down the stairs to the ground. I kept on to the archway, all the time looking up at your door. I remember the way the wind kept coming in gusts from behind me, driving the rain with it. When I reached the arch itself I actually had to hold on to the side. And then your door opened and you came out. Backwards, your back to me, and you were dragging something. It—"

Uncle Wilf broke off. "Less than two months ago. I have nightmares about it. It'll always be with me. If only I'd never found that damned letter in Brett's desk—"

"Mick's body," Howell said tonelessly, and heard his own voice as if it might have been that of a stranger, someone else in the car with them.

"I couldn't see who it was at first. You had your hands under the armpits, dragging it down backwards. I didn't see the face until you'd reached the ground and turned round. There was blood on the head . . . I recognised it then as Debroy; I remembered you introducing him to me at your school—a cricket match, I think it was. Five years before, that had been, and now—"

Uncle Wilf broke off again.

"There is something you must understand, Howell," he said earnestly. "You didn't know what you were doing. You couldn't have known, not going about it the way you did, openly, for anyone to see. Anyone could have come along at any moment. A man in control of himself, aware of his actions, would never have dragged the body down openly as you did. If ever the worst comes to the worst I will come forward and testify to that. Behaviour that speaks for itself . . .

"And that's about all. You opened one side of the garage

172

doors and dragged the body inside. Then you went back upstairs again and came down with something in your hand, and this time I could see it was a large spanner. There was blood on it. You threw it in after the body and then closed the garage up. And I went back to my car, got in and drove away."

Howell stared through the windscreen at his own car there in front of the sleek bonnet of the Aston. The sun, low now, sent slanting rays through the branches of a tree, dappling the black roof with pale golden splashes. Splashes . . . Scarlet instead of gold. Andy had said the police knew Mick hadn't been killed in the garage. If they knew that, why hadn't they been clever enough to find out where he was killed?

"Why didn't you go to the police?" Howell asked after a while.

"Why . . . ?" The older man rested his hands—long, thin white hands—on the steering wheel. "I think mainly because I owed it to the memory of the only real friend I've ever had to protect his sick son. Because I was sure that son didn't know what he was dong. And because, if I have to be honest with myself, I didn't want to become involved in murder. And there is another reason. Because I didn't actually see you kill Debroy. I can only assume that that's what happened. But for all I know Debroy might not have been alone when you stormed in with that spanner in your hand. There could have been someone else there. But there is one thing, Howell . . . If anyone else had been accused of the murder, well, then I would have taken my story to the police. I would have had no choice."

"Why are you telling me all this now?"

"Why?" Uncle Wilf said again, but this time in a very different tone. "I would have thought that was obvious. It will become so when you've had time to think. I've told you so that now you will at least know who it is who's been trying to kill you. You can't stop him making another attempt by going to the police, but you can prevent it by getting out of his reach."

Out of whose reach, for God's sake? There were only four people involved in the affair. Two of them were here in this car now, one was dead, and that left only—

"Andy?" Howell cried incredulously. "Andy Brett?"

"I've known him for five years," Uncle Wilf said. "One of the nicest young men I've ever met. Intelligent, easy to get on with, efficient in his work. If I hadn't found that letter, if I hadn't read it, I would refuse to believe it of him too. But I did find it, I read it, I told you about it, and Debroy is dead. And Brett doesn't have to be very clever to come up with the reason why he was murdered and who the killer was. You'd managed to find out that he was involved in the leakage of secrets from Trowman to Solmex. The leakage you'd been blamed for and which had meant that instead of you being in line to take over control of Trowman and become a millionaire, you'd been kicked out and forced to take a low-paid job elsewhere. No wonder you killed one of the men responsible. But the man you would really be gunning for was the villain of the piece, the traitor in the Trowman camp who did the actual selling of the secrets. Debroy, before you killed him, couldn't have told you who that someone was, otherwise you'd have denounced him in order to clear your name. You don't know yet who he is, you might have suspicions, you're certainly on his trail. You must be stopped before you go any further. And there's only the one way to stop you. And for all Brett knows, you might feel like doing the same to him as you did to his partner. Why he should have waited until two months after Debroy's death before making the first attempt, I don't know. Unless it is that something has happened within the last few days to make him think you were on to him."

It all fitted. It all made sense. Events as Howell saw them were capable of no other explanation.

"I tried to see him," he said stonily. "I went to his place. He wouldn't let me in, wouldn't listen to me. The first attempt was made the next morning. I never associated one thing with the other. Why should I have done? He must have thought that I wanted to—"

"What are you going to do?" Uncle Wilf asked.

Do . . . ? What could he do? He couldn't go to the police. There was nobody he could turn to for help. He was on his

174

own. On his own in an alien time that had already started to turn into a nightmare before this little lot had broken.

"Money," Uncle Wilf said. "How are you fixed for money?" The brief case. "I'm all right," Howell said.

"Although it might not be a very good idea to leave the country. That's why I asked, Howell. In case that was what you had in mind. But leaving might be seen as a confession of guilt. There's one thing I have to say. If the police ever did come to me I wouldn't be able to trust myself not to tell them what I saw that night. I wouldn't want to tell them . . . I'm no good at this sort of thing."

Despite himself, Howell smiled a little. "I know." He reached to open the car door. "Thanks for everything, anyway." He tried not to sound sarcastic.

"Where are you going?" the other asked with great concern.

"Back to London." Howell shrugged. "After that, God knows."

"Let me know what you do decide. And Howell—" Uncle Wilf leaned towards him. "Please see a doctor. This thing, this—this hallucination, that you think has happened to you . . . It's only in your mind. It must have been coming on for some time. Then you reached breaking point. Promise me you'll go to a doctor, a psychiatrist. No need to be ashamed; no need to tell him anything, only that you've been overworking. Promise me—"

Howell smiled down at him. "Give my love to Aunt Meg," he said, slammed the door and turned to walk the few paces to his own car, the small battered black saloon, its interior a few cubic feet of petrol-stinking squalor after the leather luxuriance of the Aston Martin. He reversed in two clumsy manoeuvres, the bonnet rearing up against the hedge, a branch lashing against the mottled-yellow windscreen, and accelerated away, lifting his hand in passing to the still stationary Aston, its owner sitting unhappily in solitary splendour.

He tried to clear his mind of everything, to empty it completely. The time for thinking, for working out what to do, would come later. And for wondering why, if he now had the full history of those damned five years, down to the last sordid detail, he was still here in 1974.

He remembered little of the drive back to London. It was dark when he swung in through the archway. As always, the courtyard was deserted. Step by tired step he climbed the metal stairway. The door he had left on the catch for Tina was now locked. Nine o'clock, he had told her in his note. It was almost eleven. She would have returned all right, but he very much doubted whether she would still be waiting for him. Unlocking the door he stepped into the hall. The lounge door was open a little way; the lounge light was on. So she was still here. Pushing the door wide open he stepped into the room.

Tina sat on the settee, on the very edge of the settee, knees tight together, hands clasped, gaze on the doorway, obviously waiting for his return, but oddly, not smiling at seeing him, instead looking to be worried and concerned. And she wasn't alone. It was the way her gaze suddenly shifted, so that now she was looking over his shoulder, behind him, at something behind him, that made Howell stop and turn. And almost bump into the two men who had moved up silently from either side of the doorway to stand almost touching him.

Wharton, who was supposed to be a doctor, took hold of his arm in a firm grip. The big man with the ballooning shoulders and evil doll-puppet face had a syringe in one pudgy hand, held ready, needle poised, ready for the flesh of Howell's arm to be exposed by Wharton stripping off the jacket and pulling up the shirt sleeve.

Smoothly, quickly, efficiently, almost as if rehearsed. Before Howell, weary and startled, knew what was happening.

Not a word spoken.

The needle stung.

The room swayed. The light dimmed. Blackness came.

13

A CIRCLE OF TINY PEOPLE ON TINY CHAIRS, boys and girls, and he one of them. Singing—what was the song—a children's carol, for the first Christmas he could remember.

And then the soft feel and clovey smell of Plasticine. Figures set out on a small square of wood. An elephant, a man with a whip, a clown.

And then—how old now?—seven—really grown-up, and the fall from the farm gate and the long black splinter, drawn satisfyingly from pink flesh like a sword from a sheath.

Budders, then; Buddleigh Hall School, and this, his first day there, a nightmare, strange and terrifying. And his first night in the lonely twilight world of the dormitory, sobbing, his soot-streaked face pressed into the pillow.

Older, almost a man now. And this his room at school, his private, prefect's room with its workhouse-green walls and furniture polish smell. Sitting on the solitary hard-backed chair, looking at the narrow window, waiting . . . Mother and Dad somewhere on their way in the black Austin Princess. Go down to meet them—Mother in her everlasting blue, the old man in his idea of correct country wear. Meet them and talk and laugh and bring them back up here and then tell them what he had decided to do. And which would it be—into the firm as Mother wanted, or the Oxford the old man had set his heart on?

Still older, and certainly a man now. Desks, and people working at those desks. But not too busy to stop their typing and paper rustling and telephone calling to look up, the room suddenly silent, everything and everyone watching and listening. Listening to Dad ordering him to get out, to get the hell out of it—don't ever come back.

Shapes dissolving, reforming. Wind and rain and night-time. Driving back through the rain, the shining pavements deserted, each street lamp a lonely blurred golden star. Through the archway and into the courtyard. His head aching. Tired . . . No idea of the time; no memory of where he had been, what he had been doing. Swaying on his feet as he went to open the white ghost-shapes of the garage doors—not locked—why bother? No strangers ever came in here.

The door, one side of it, opening, grating a little over the cobblestones. Light flooding in from the car headlamps. Like spot-lights on a stage, all trained on the thing lying there on the oil-stained concrete—an old sack, he fancied at first—where had it come from? And then his vision cleared, and he could see what it was.

Blood. On his clothes, on his hands. Blood everywhere.

A nightmare. Worse than that first day at school.

Shapes melting, dissolving, reforming.

Another room, large, opulent, luxurious. As unlike his tiny cell at school as one could possibly imagine, and yet in some strange way linked with it. He knew why that was, the knowledge was there in his mind, but he couldn't reach it. Very badly he wanted to remember. Suddenly it became very important he remember.

Howell opened his eyes, and the memory of the room became the reality of the room.

For a while he remained still, half-lying in the deep leather armchair, quite content to gaze about him, remembering the paintings and statuettes, the bookcase, the wine-red drapes and the porcelain figurines in the tall glass cabinet by the curtained window. Curtained now because it was night, there was darkness out there, not the bright sunlight of his last awakening here.

And finally his slow-drifting gaze came to rest on the paper-littered expanse of the red-wood desk, and the man who had just resumed his seat behind it. A huge, bloated man, with tiny doll features set in puffy pink-and-white flesh.

There was a name to go with that gross body, that no longer evil, no-longer-to-be-feared puppet's face.

"Poitier," Howell said, and a certain look of anxiety faded, and the big man smiled and nodded like a Chinese mandarin figure.

"Which means you are back again, Mr. Trowman," he said, a high-pitched voice that fitted the face but not the body. "I won't disguise my relief. I must apologise for the—ah—dramatic way in which we assailed you. We felt we had little choice. The young lady, Miss Martin, had told us you had made enemies of us. Which meant, we felt almost sure, you would have resisted any attempt on our part to bring you here. And I didn't want to risk attempting the process of—ah—rehabilitation in the unsuitable surroundings of your own home. You are aware of what happened to you?"

"I've a fairly good idea," Howell told him, his mind on other things.

"You have undergone what must have been a strange and disturbing experience. We must discuss it at length. But not now, not at this late hour. You will be wishing to return to your flat. May I first offer you something to drink?"

"Thanks. I don't think so." Howell looked at his watch. Ten minutes after midnight. The ormolu clock on the mantel of the Adam fireplace confirmed that. Late, but not too late for what he had to do. What could wait for a more reasonable hour, but which he wanted to do right away.

"May I use your phone?" he asked Poitier.

The huge man nodded, his eyes curious. "Help yourself, Mr. Trowman." He indicated the centre one of the three telephones on the desk. "I had my housekeeper put out a vacuum of hot chocolate and some sandwiches—"

Howell pushed himself to his feet from the depths of the

chair. It took him a few moments to remember a certain number. Then: "Blake Street police station? My name is Howell Trowman, and I'm speaking from Gladwyn Place, S.W. nineteen. Number"—he had to think again—"forty. I want to speak to Inspector Mellor. And before whoever it was at the other end could reply: "If he's not there, get in touch with him. Tell him I know who murdered Martin Debroy. I'll be—"

He paused to look enquiry at Poitier, who nodded. "Be my guest, and welcome, Mr. Trowman."

"I'll be waiting here at Gladwyn Place," Howell finished, and replaced the receiver.

"Interesting," the big man observed almost conversationally. "You are going to stir things up, Mr. Trowman. I have the feeling you have quite a night ahead of you. Perhaps it would be just as well if you were to take advantage of my offer of refreshment."

It was a little after six, clear bright sunlight, milk bottles jangling, a newspaper boy whistling, when a police car dropped Howell off by the arched entrance to the courtyard. The driver, a moustached sergeant, leaned out of the open window, hand raised to peaked cap in a half-salute, smiling. "You'll have some sleep to catch up on, Mr. Trowman. Head down for you now, I reckon?"

"I suppose so," Howell told him. But he didn't feel at all tired. That would come later when this feeling of exhilaration had worn off. There would be an anti-climax; there always was, for everything.

His old car was the only thing in the courtyard. It was rarely he saw anything of his neighbours. One thing, the woman with the poodle—a hyphenated name—Watson-Hughes—at least she wouldn't need to look scared to death next time she had to pass him. By then she would have read in the papers how Debroy's real murderer had confessed and been arrested.

Howell climbed the grilled iron staircase and fitted his key in the front door lock. No need now to keep pestering the landlord about having that door repainted, the whole place decorated. He would only be living here a few more days now, just until he had found himself something better.

For a startled, stupid moment he didn't recognise the girl who lay sleeping on the settee in the long room. But then Tina's hair had changed its familiar pattern, falling to completely cover her face, and she was wearing a skirt, not the slacks he had become used to—he had forgotten she had gone home to change—now she was wearing a brief apology for a skirt that exposed legs it was a crime to cover with anything, and a high-necked, bare-armed scarlet blouse affair.

She stirred under his gaze, stretched, opened her eyes and blinked up at the ceiling, frowning, obviously getting her bearings. And then, about to swing her legs to the floor, only then did she see him watching her from the doorway.

"Howie!" Her delight at seeing him brought her in one swift movement to her feet. But then she stopped, doubtful, anxious, apprehensive. "It *is* you, Howie?"

He had been waiting for something like that. "Both of us, Tina." He came smiling towards her. "Two for the price of one." And he put his hands on her shoulders, then let them slip down to her waist as she leaned towards him. They kissed for the first time, gently, naturally, as if it were something they had been in the habit of doing all their lives.

She stepped back, out of his arms, looking up at the sun-filled skylights. "But it's morning. Have you only just got back, Howie?"

"This very minute."

"Where have you been till now, then? What have you been doing?" And before he could reply: "What about breakfast—have you had anything to eat?"

"It's only six o'clock yet." But because he knew she was always happy and at home in a kitchen: "I'd like some coffee."

She paused in the kitchen doorway, turned slowly to look at him, doubtful again.

"Last night, Howie . . . It was through me they were here, you know. I went to find out if Wharton really was a doctor. He was, and he told me that something had happened to you—I couldn't make out what—to do with your mind, and you must be seen to as fast as possible. He phoned that other man, the big man—Poitier—a psychiatrist, he said. They came back here with me. I wanted to help you—"

"You did perfectly right," he assured her warmly.

"Well, thank heaven for that. So what's it all about, Howie? I still can't make any sense of it at all. Only that you've been ill—"

"Coffee," he reminded her, smiling, and followed her into the kitchen, there to drag out the stool and sit astride it, one leg swinging. His face itched a little. Shaving could wait, though.

"Don't just sit there looking smug and self-complacent," Tina said, busy filling a kettle. "Do you want me to burst with curiosity? Or is it you just don't want to finally have to admit that I was right about you all the time, and you were wrong?"

He knew what she meant. "I wasn't wrong," he told her blandly. "It all happened exactly as I told you. I was brought here from nineteen sixty-nine. One moment I was sitting in my room at school, the next I was in Mr. Poitier's consulting room in Gladwyn Place."

She stared at him over a match struck ready to light the stove. "But that's impossible!" The flame touched her fingers and she shook it out. "You still can't believe that? Howie . . . They said they were taking you away to do something to you to make you yourself again. To cure you, I thought. Mr. Poitier used a word—'abreaction'—I didn't know what it meant. I thought it must be some kind of treatment. You're not teasing me, Howie, pretending you're still—?"

"Still off my nut?" he finished for her, and threw back his head to laugh. "No, I wouldn't do that, Tina. I never was a nut case, anyway. No hallucinations or anything like that. When I told you I'd been wafted here from five years in the past I was telling you the truth. And not only the truth as I saw it, but as it actually was. But only part of it, and that's where the catch is. That's why it doesn't make sense, why it seems impossible. But once you know the full story, then it'll be a very different affair.

"It actually does start on that day back at school when I

was sweet seventeen and I had to make up my mind one way or another, and I was worried sick in case I made the wrong choice. The sort of thing that leaves a lasting impression on the mind. Well, I finally decided to do as Mother wanted and go straight into the firm. Dad took it far better than I thought. I have the feeling he must have had some idea just how ill he was. I joined the firm, and a few weeks later someone started leaking our trade secrets to Solmex. Try as we would, we couldn't find out who was responsible, even though Dad engaged a firm of enquiry agents. It couldn't go on, we were losing too much money. Then I got my bright idea. We'd got nowhere at our end, so how about if we could wangle a spy into the enemy camp? Fair enough, but there was no one we could trust. Except me. Dad wasn't all that keen on the idea, but I talked him into it—God, if only I'd known what I was letting myself in for. But I think I wanted a chance to prove myself to him, you know? Let him see I could be trusted to cope with things, that I'd be capable of taking over from him when the time came.

"Well, he finally agreed. We didn't let anyone else in on it, not even Mother, in case she spilled it to Uncle Wilf. We were in such a state we couldn't even trust him. We staged a series of arguments, ending up with a real snorter, acted out in the main office in front of everyone, with me being given my marching orders.

"As planned, I went staight to Mick Debroy. It worked out better than I'd hoped. I didn't even have to ask him to help me find digs, or a job with Solmex. He offered both. And as for Solmex—they were only too damn' pleased to be able to say they had the son of their biggest competitor working behind one of their menial desks. Something to crow about.

"Dad kept in touch with me, of course. And after a bit it became clear that the leakages had stopped at the same time as I had left. Which was rather disturbing. The leakages had started when I arrived, ended when I left. It looked like someone was deliberately gunning for me. And there was no doubt now that everyone at Trowman were as sure as could be I was the traitor. Which was just what we had wanted them to believe, but which still wasn't all that pleasant for me. It's not a nice feeling knowing that all your friends, everyone, even your own mother, believes you to be a first-class stinking rat who's sold even your old man down the river. After a while it began to get on top of me. I started taking tablets to help me sleep nights. And I was getting nowhere fast trying to find the real traitor's contact at Solmex. And there had to be one; you don't deal directly with the big noises where that sort of thing's concerned. The bosses take damn' good care to keep their lily-white hands clean and unsullied. They probably didn't even know who the go-between was. I had a fairly good idea that the person I was after was just an ordinary insignificant staff member."

He broke off as Tina brought him a cup of coffee.

"It's like something on the telly," she said. "Agents, espionage . . . I didn't know such things really do happen."

"There's no romance to it," Howell said bitterly. "If being a spy makes you feel like I felt, they're bloody well welcome to it. I never want to go through anything like that again.

"Well, like I said"—sipping the coffee—"I was getting no place fast. And then I got a break. I went into Mick Debroy's office to ask him something. He wasn't there. The phone rang just as I was leaving. A voice said: 'Your call to Gretton has come through now, Mr. Debroy.' I had the sense to mumble something and then replace the receiver.

"I could think of only the one reason why Mick should be calling someone at Gretton. Gretton *is* Trowman Chemicals. Whoever it was he wanted to talk to had to be a Trowman employee. Got him, I thought. And after some thinking, I had a fairly good idea who the traitor at Trowman was. It was all to do with that day back at school when it all started. Mick Debroy told me he had got himself a job with Solmex, and he did go to work for them a few weeks later, attending university part time. And Andy Brett, that same day, asked me to ask Dad if a spot could be found for him at Trowman. As I saw it, the two of them had worked the whole thing out while they were still at school. How to get rich in one easy lesson. Start up your own business of selling and buying trade secrets.

"But I didn't want to tell Dad until I had proof. I went out after Debroy first, hating his very guts for what he had done to the old man, what he had done to me. Two years of misery, of everyone being against me—that's what I'd had to go through because of him. The first chance I got, I went through the things in his bedroom here. I found his bank statements, but they showed nothing big had been paid for the last three years. And he must have been paid for his part in it. And then I found the brief case, hidden at the back of his wardrobe. He was that sure of himself, that sure I'd never go prying in his things, that the key was in the lock. It was full of money, of course. That clinched Debroy. Now for Andy Brett.

"And the next day, the old man died. Nobody told me, nobody wrote to me. I read it in the paper like any other news item the morning after. There was a picture of him. Not a very good one. I went to the funeral. That really brought it home to me where I stood. Not a soul spoke to me, not even Uncle Wilf and Aunt Meg, not even Mother. They were all blaming me for having hastened Dad's end. If I'd had Debroy there in front of me, I'd have strangled him with my bare hands.

"That really put the lid on things. With Dad dead, my only hope of clearing my name and going back to Trowman was to come up with the name of the real traitor. I wasn't far off breaking point—I knew that. I had a blackout at the office. Then another, here at the flat, and they sent for Wharton. He put me on another sort of drug, stronger than that I'd been taking. It didn't help much. I had more blackouts, some lasting quite a while, with no idea when I came round what I'd been doing.

"And then—" Howell paused. "I was in my car, driving back here. I didn't know where I'd been to, what I'd been doing. It was night, and it was raining and windy. I can remember climbing out of the car and opening the garage door. There was something lying on the floor. I didn't know it was a body, Debroy's body, until I'd touched it and got blood on my hands. And so then I had no way of telling if there had been blood on my hands before I touched the body. I could have killed Debroy during one of my blackouts, driven away, recovered, driven back again. Because of the way I'd come to feel about him, I knew that that was more than a possibility. But I had no intention of giving myself up so long as there was any doubt. There was no motive for the police to latch on to. But there would be when they came to search the flat, as they would be bound to do, and found the money. I had to hide the brief case. I asked Pete to look after it for me. A risk, but there was no time to do anything else. I had to report the death to the police straight away, otherwise, with their way of finding things out, they'd want to know why I'd delayed.

"They came and went, the police—an Inspector Mellor in charge. They found nothing to prove I had anything to do with the murder. The papers were sure I was the killer; they howled like a pack of wolves for my blood. Mellor was very decent to me. He told me they didn't think I was their man. For several reasons—no motive, for a start; and Debroy hadn't actually been killed in the garage, and the spanner used wasn't of the kind generally supplied with either my make of car or Debroy's, still in the garage at one side. There were other reasons, and he asked me to keep them to myself for the time being, that he'd only told me because he knew I must be worried.

"It helped, I suppose, knowing the police weren't gunning for me. But judging by the papers, everyone else seemed to think I was as guilty as hell. And the trouble was, I didn't even know myself. I went to see Wharton again, giving as an excuse that my blackouts were getting worse. I wanted to find out if it was medically possible for me to have committed murder without knowing anything about it. I didn't ask him that outright, of course, but he may have guessed. Anyway, he said it wasn't his field and that I ought to see a consultant psychiatrist. He made an appointment for me to see Mr. Poitier. Ten-thirty in the morning, Saturday, July the sixth.

"I drove out to Gladwyn Place. It took me some time to find a place to park, so I was late for the appointment. He saw me straight away. Just an ordinary sort of room, a desk and a filing cabinet, no couch. He had me sit in a big easy chair. He said he'd read my case history and that on the face of it it looked to him as if my blackouts were being caused by my subconscious trying to blot out something in my past it would like to forget. He told me what he was going to do—give me a drug, just a sedative—then hypnotise me and then get me to go right back as far as I could remember. 'Abreaction,' he called the process of going back like that. He said he needed my help first. What was the very earliest thing I could remember? Singing Christmas carols in kindergarten, I told him. And then he wanted highlights in my life, things, good or bad, that stood out in my memory without having to dig for them. Like the time I fell off a gate and got a whopping great splinter in my leg. Like my first day at Buddleigh School—miserable as hell, that was. Milestones, he called them. And then pressed a bell and a nurse in a Hollywood get-up came in with a hypodermic syringe and he jabbed it in my arm, and I was half-way gone before he started in on the hypnosis bit.

"I was singing carols at the top of my tiny voice; I was rolling Plasticine into all sorts of shapes; I was pulling out that splinter and leaving a scar you can still see to this day if you're that way inclined. Are you?"

"I'll take your word for it," Tina said. "Go on."

"I was sobbing my heart out on the dormitory pillow. And then I was sitting in my room at school wracking my brains as to what to do for the best. Which you don't need me to remind you is where we came in.

"But I was out, of course, well and truly out; and so we have to take Mr. Poitier's word for what happened. He told me all about it last night while we were waiting for the police to show up. And apologised for what after all wasn't his fault. He brought me up to that day at school in 'sixty-nine, and then I began to show signs of distress—his words—I became agitated. I got so worked up he tried moving me away, but I refused to budge. The only thing to do was pump more sedative into me, enough to calm me down so that he could get me under control again. He rang for the nurse, but she didn't answer. He knew that wherever she'd gone, she'd soon be back, but he felt he couldn't take the risk of me getting even more distressed. So he took the lesser risk of leaving me alone while he went to fill a syringe himself. He was only away a few minutes, but during that time I'd woke myself up and walked out—still living my schoolday memory—not only believing myself to be only seventeen, but actually only just that age. So far as I was concerned, the five years I'd lost had never existed.

"Poitier ran out into the street, but I'd gone. He rang up Wharton to tell him what had happened, and the two of them set about getting me back without alarming me in any way. Poitier said he felt pretty sure he knew just what had happened, that I had become displaced, as he put it. It would have worn off in time, he told me, probably gradually. But knowing that I must be finding life confusing, to say the least, he wanted to get me back to normal as quickly as possible. Which he finally did do last night, by putting me under again, then making me go right back to the beginning, and then work forward from there, right through the tricky period up to the present. And here I am, both of me, and I'm grateful to you, Tina, for having brought them here last night."

Howell held out his empty cup. "And if there's any more coffee left in the pot, I'd be grateful for that."

There was, but it had cooled. "I'll make some more," Tina said. And smugly, as she lighted the gas again: "I told you all along you'd been hypnotised, didn't I?"

"So you did," he agreed, allowing her her small moment of triumph, his still to come.

She became indignant. "A mistake, Howie! You went through all that just because a doctor slipped up."

"A calculated risk that came unstuck," he corrected. "I don't see he had any choice. And anyway, I'm not complaining. Because of what happened, things have worked out very nicely. Did I tell you the police arrested Debroy's murderer last night? The same bloke who tried to do me in. Twice. But you don't know about the second one, do you?"

He started telling her about the farm, but, more interested in the murderer's identity, she cut him short impatiently. "For heaven's sake, Howie—who was it?"

Time for his moment of triumph. "Ask me how the police got on to him," he urged.

She obliged. "How did they get on to him?"

"I told them," he said complacently. "At least, I told them who I was almost sure it was, and I told them what to do to get

188

him to break down if he was the one. He's that sort of man. The slightest chink in his armour and he comes to pieces.

"I told the police to go to Gretton, to the house where I used to live—remember?—and go in the garage and open a certain tool chest. And then take what they found in there to Mr. Sinclair, otherwise good old Uncle Wilf, and ask him how Debroy's old school scarf came to be hidden in his garage. Which—"

"You mean, the man you call your Uncle Wilf?" Tina broke in.

"Which they did," he continued, nodding, "and bingo, he collapsed like a burst balloon. It seems there was blood on it, which helped matters. I came across it, the scarf, when I was looking for something to open the french window with, and I thought it must be one of mine. I didn't know then that it wasn't my home any more, and that when Mother moved out, she took everything away with her, lock, stock and barrel.

"So whose scarf was it? Only two names on the list—Andy Brett and Mick Debroy. No reason why one of Andy's scarfs should be hidden in the garage. But I could think of a good reason why Debroy's scarf should be there. My guess was that he had actually been killed there in Uncle Wilf's garage, and that Uncle Wilf was the murderer. That's how I had it figured and that's how it was.

"Mr. Poitier let me hang on at his consulting rooms last night until Inspector Mellor had been out to Gretton to do his stuff. I didn't want to come back here until the whole thing was all cut and dried, all tied up, no loose ends.

"When it was all over, Mellor rang to give me the gist of Uncle Wilf's statement. Poor Aunt Meg—God knows how she's taken it. She knew nothing about it, of course. And in a way I even feel sorry for Uncle Wilf. Even though he was the cause of my having to live through five years I'd much rather hadn't happened. He collapsed last night; they took him to hospital, not prison.

"Weak, unreliable, apt to panic at the slightest thing. I think I may have told you that he and Dad started the firm together and then, when things went wrong, Uncle Wilf threw a panic and wanted out. Then when things looked up again, Dad took him back into the firm. But not as a partner. And that's what Uncle Wilf really wanted—to become partner again. Not so much for the money as the prestige and power. They say that folk with inferiority complexes always go all out after power.

"He knew from Mother that Dad wasn't well, that he'd been to see various specialists. The time was ripe, he felt, to ask to be reinstated, after all the years, as partner. Dad said he'd think about it. That was before he knew of my decision to join the firm instead of going to Oxford. When he did know it, he changed his mind about Uncle Wilf. I think he knew he hadn't all that long to live, and was secretly relieved at my decision to join the firm. I would take over after a period of intensive training, and there'd be no need to make Uncle Wilf a partner after all.

"Which made Uncle Wilf mad, to say the least. If he couldn't get power one way, he'd get it another, by being the one to topple the Trowman empire. And he'd have his revenge for being pushed aside for a school kid. And he'd make money in the process. He contacted the only employee of Solmex that he knew. He'd met Debroy when he'd come to visit me at school. Debroy always did have an eye to the main chance. He took this one with both hands, acting as intermediary, helping himself to his rake-off each time money changed hands, keeping the loot in that brief case so that nobody would start wondering why his bank account had suddenly started to blossom.

"Well, that went on for three years, until I left after that fake quarrel with the old man. Uncle Wilf, back in the line for a partnership, called off the arrangement. Which Debroy, steadily building up a tidy little fortune, didn't like one little bit. If he couldn't continue getting the money one way, well, there was always another, if even more unsavoury, way."

"Blackmail?" Tina guessed, and Howell nodded. "Reasonable amounts at first. And then Dad died, Uncle Wilf took over, and good old Debroy stepped up his demands accordingly. And Uncle Wilf got really desperate.

"The murder wasn't premeditated. A spur of the moment

job. Debroy came down to Gretton to personally enforce his new demands. By now he must have felt he knew the sort of man he was dealing with, easily intimidated. Uncle Wilf took him to the garage to talk—he didn't want Aunt Meg to see Debroy, and it was raining, too wet to talk outside. So there they were, and in the middle of it all Uncle Wilf spotted the spanner lying on the bench, picked it up and swung it. And that was it. He carried the body to Debroy's own car, drove it back here to the flat, put the car away in the garage and arranged the body on the floor, put the spanner near by—no finesse—took a taxi back to Gretton and hoped I'd be blamed. He must have sweated when the weeks went by without me being arrested. No wonder he looked sick and worried. Andy thought it was because he couldn't take the responsibility that had been thrust at him. How wrong can you be?"

"Coffee," Tina said, and refilled his cup. "I'd better start getting breakfast ready." She turned from opening the cupboard. "I suppose you'll go back to your own firm now?"

"You are looking," he informed her with mock pomposity, "at a millionaire. Or the makings of one. It'll take us some time to get back on our feet again."

She curtsied, rasher of bacon in hand. "I'm suitably impressed." And then pulled a face. "No, I'm not. You're no different from what you were yesterday. Howie, what does it feel like, you know, being yourself again?"

"Me and me." He considered the thing. "It's a bit odd in a way. Remembering how I felt yesterday. It's like growing up five years overnight. Going to bed a schoolboy, waking up a hardened businessman. You know. Although I think I'd already started to catch up with myself."

"I know you had," Tina said.

"Concentrated living." His half-smile faded. "A nightmare while it lasted. At least, that's what it had started to turn into towards the end, when I was alone and I thought I was stuck here with no hope of ever getting back to my own time and place.

"And yet, you know, if it had never happened, if I hadn't woke myself up into a time where I didn't belong, I'd still be number one rat, no friends left, everyone against me, some hating me, others screaming for my blood. And with damn' little hope of ever clearing myself. I mean, who'd ever have believed my story?

"Breaking into what I thought was my home was the turning point. Uncle Wilf was sure I'd got on to him and had come looking for the proof so that I could expose him. That's why he tried to kill me. And damn' near managed it at the farm." Howell shivered. "I won't forget that cellar in a hurry.

"And then, when he found out the real reason why I'd broken in, he tried to make me think I was the murderer myself, that I'd done Debroy in without knowing what I was doing. I suppose he hoped I'd either give myself up or commit suicide or leave the country. Or else go mad or something. I was just about ready to believe him, too. And that's something else I could very well have done without—that last drive from Gretton back to London, not knowing whether I was a murderer or not."

Howell drained his cup and set it down.

"I'm not likely to forget any of it in a hurry," he said.